Anthro

By Andy Joy

Dorrance Publishing Co
585 Alpha Drive
Pittsburgh, PA 15238
Visit our website at www.dorrancebookstore.com

ISBN: 979-8-8868-3186-3
eISBN: 979-8-8868-3759-9

Prologue: The Rodrick Virus

It happened quickly, like the blink of an eye, but not many noticed it when it happened. He had planned it perfectly. Waited till the perfect moment and then he changed the world. Some would say later that it was for the better, others for the worse, but he had changed it, no one could argue that. Dr. Francis Rodrick was at one time a highly respected scientist specializing in biology and genetics. A prodigy of sorts. The kind of man that makes a name for himself early on in his career and then disappear into some secret government project.

That was what happened to Rodrick, until he was suddenly removed from his position and stripped of all his clearances and titles. Even those who worked closely with him didn't know why he had been throw out, but he disappeared for the second time. Out of the anonymity of government secrets and into the anonymity of the public.

Of course the public knew nothing. There was no public record of him since he had graduated college, but that was common for the top-secret scientists the government employed. And he would use this fact to his advantage, and the government would rue the day they let him walk away free.

Even they didn't fully understand what he intended to do. If they had, they surely would have tried to stop him. But his research and plans were in their infancy when the government had discovered what he had been experimenting with. And they quickly disposed of him on the spot and destroyed what little he had accomplished. It did little to stop him though as he carried on with his plans in secret and on his own.

It took him years to develop it, years to perfect it, and years to plan for it. But he was always a patient man and he had nothing but time. To this day, it isn't known how exactly he was able to develop it, let alone afford the equipment and materials it required. Rodrick had done something that was thought impossible, implausible, and even ridiculous by anyone with even an ounce of sense or scientific knowledge. But he proved them all wrong and killed most of them when he revealed his masterpiece to the world.

One quiet spring morning, he set his carefully laid plans into motion. And with the push of a button, it was over, and the course of history was changed forever. He had rigged multiple small but powerful black-market rockets with his masterpiece and sent them screaming into the upper atmosphere, where they detonated and released it onto the world. It would, of course, take several days for it to spread from the upper atmosphere to the ground below. But releasing it so high would ensure that the winds of the world would carry it to every corner of the planet.

He waited two weeks, then drove a tanker truck full of his creation into the middle of Times Square, where he revealed what he had created.

With a smile on his face and speaking calmly but excitedly into a microphone mounted onto the side of the truck, he started to explain, "Hello, everyone! My name is Dr. Francis Rodrick! And in this tank..." he slapped the side of the tank, "...is a biological virus of my own creation."

He smiled as several news crews approached with cameras pointed at him, broadcasting his message live on the air. Several police cars came screeching to a stop all around him, and several officers jumped out.

They pointed their guns at him, but he held up a cylindrical remote control and warned, "Now, now, gentleman..." he grinned at the officers nearest him, "...one push of this button and it'll be released...let me explain! This virus will, upon entering a person's system, begin to alter their very DNA. In a very painful process that will take several weeks. Many, as you might expect, will not survive the alterations and will die a slow, painful death..."

At his words, several of the people closest to Rodrick began to frantically try to get away from him. Others just stood still or sat in their vehicles in shock and not totally comprehending what they were hearing.

Rodrick looked directly at the cameras that were still pointed at him as he continued, "However, those that do survive will find their bodies very different from what they were. You see...my virus alters human DNA and introduces more...bestial DNA to them. In effect those that survive will be a combination of both human...and animal. A perfect organism...if I do say so myself..." Rodrick grinned again as more people began to flee and more police arrived and shouted orders at him, which he ignored and continued speaking, "...Yes, but perfection has a cost. Limbs will disintegrate, break, and reform; muscles will stretch, deform, and tear, extra limbs, tails and such will painfully sprout and form..."

Even more people were fleeing now, and Rodrick was enjoying seeing them run in terror. Some of the police officers were visibly shaking as well. None of them realized they were all, almost certainly, already infected.

He was interrupted by an officer with a megaphone who asked, "What are your demands?! You do you want?!"

"Demands?" Rodrick repeated, smiling at the few cameras still pointed at him, and laughed, "I want to change the world!"

And with those words, he hit the button and several valves on the tank opened spraying clouds of thick white smoke over the area. Everyone, even the police officers, ran screaming from the clouds, but it was too late as the smoke enveloped everyone. Not that it really mattered either way, but Rodrick enjoyed hearing their terrified screams as they desperately tried to avoid it.

Of course he was promptly arrested and interrogated by the government. He told them again, in detail, what would happen. It would come to pass just as he described it, every horrible aspect. It was exactly as he had planned.

The Rodrick Virus, as his creation was later dubbed, would change the world. In the first six months after he released it, it would kill roughly half of all human life on the planet.

As he would tell his interrogators, "Even a brainless insect could simply kill people."

That wasn't his end goal. No, Rodrick had merely culled the weak and gave the world "breathing room" as he described it. How exactly he was able to create the virus, or any details about how exactly it worked, he wouldn't divulge.

Scientists worked tirelessly to decipher his methods but were never able to. Just as he had stated, the people who were infected began to change. Physical forms varied wildly, but all had one thing in common: all resembled a combination of human and animal. Every animal from the lowly mouse to the mighty lion were represented in these new creations from the Virus. However, these poor souls kept their minds and didn't devolve into the animals they resembled.

Many initially called them Furries. A term they refused because of its association with humans who wanted to become a hybrid of human and animal, or at least enjoyed the artistic aspects of human-animal hybrids. Anthropomorphic, which is usually used to describe something nonhuman with human characteristics, was the word chosen to describe them instead. Despite the moniker being technically incorrect because they had been human before the Virus rather than just displaying human characteristics. It was what stuck. The word being somewhat long and unwieldly, many began shortening it to what the afflicted would be called from then on, Anthros.

Chapter 1: One Month After Outbreak

Jack Towzer was an average young man with brown hair and eyes. He possessed no discernible or unique features to speak of, being of average height and weight. Generally he faded into the background when in a crowd, too.

However, what did stand out about Jack was his personality, being overly kind and helpful almost to a fault, as well as being a hard worker who wasn't overly serious or up tight, at least not when it came to most things. Perhaps his biggest fault, however, had to be his lack of confidence. It was this lack of confidence that was the reason he still worked at his dead-end job where he cut grass for the local school.

He liked his job well enough, that wasn't the problem; the problem was he had always dreamed of being a farmer and owning a farm of his own. Of course he knew he had time, he was only twenty-four after all. But he still felt as though he hadn't made any progress since he graduated high school. The thought of working at his current job for the rest of his life made him depressed.

Farms were expensive though, and he was having trouble saving the money. Even if he saved the money, he had to face the possibility of failure. It wasn't enough to just be able to afford the farm, he had to be able to do the necessary work and make a profit doing it.

Jack shook the depressing thoughts from his head and focused on the small TV in the corner. The morning news was on, and the anchorman on the screen was talking about the Virus, like everyone else.

"...new cases of the Rodrick Virus continue to appear. Experts studying the Virus are divided on what the next measures should be, to both stop the spread and help those already infected..."

It had been the only thing on the news for the last month. He wasn't surprised and had gotten somewhat used to seeing the broadcasts. Although it seemed like every day the Virus got worse and worse. The anchorman was now talking about the attack on Times Square.

"Police and law enforcement are still trying to determine a motive for the terrorist attack perpetrated by the self-proclaimed creator of the Virus. But, given the information they've already attained from Rodrick himself since he was taken into custody. It seems the attack was most likely fueled by either revenge or resentment for some perceived wrong in the past. Or a misguided attempt at some kind of notoriety or publicity. Although it's still unclear and a full psychological evaluation has been ordered by investigators but hasn't been released to the public yet..."

Jack had lost count of how many times he had seen it. Or how many different "experts" had talked about it and what the madman known as Francis Rodrick claimed it would do to people. As time progressed and more people got sick, the first mutations had started.

Scientists and doctors, when talking about it, divided the Rodrick Virus into an initial stage, Stage One, and an advanced stage, Stage Two. The first stage was what was killing people and was marked by all the horrible symptoms one would expect as the Virus tried to alter the infected person's body but failed. Stage Two was what happened when the Virus was actually successful at mutating people into what were being referred to as anthropomorphic beings, or Anthros for short.

News stations everywhere weren't shy about showing how people where changing either, and soon every broadcast had some new terrible story about someone who was turning into a fish, bird, or insect-like beast. They even showed how the Virus progressed and how painful it was. Jack felt sorry for the poor people he saw on those broadcasts.

Just as concerning was the fact that, despite all the safety precautions and quarantines, the Virus continued to spread rapidly. Scientists and doctors from all over the world were trying to solve the mystery. All they knew though was that it was spread by contact with infected people. Currently on the news, the anchorman was now talking to an expert on infectious diseases about the spread of the Virus, "Dr. Wall, as a scientist who has studied infectious diseases, and specifically how they spread... why haven't the quarantine measures and other regulations that the government put in place slowed the spread of the Rodrick Virus? In fact there has been a steady increase in the number of infected people since the Times Square attack...what do you think is causing the government's protective measures to fail?" the anchorman asked, and Dr. Wall responded, "Well honestly this Virus is unlike anything we've ever seen obviously... but my colleagues and I believe that the failure isn't with the government or their policies on the matter. No, I would put the blame for this utter catastrophe on the public before anyone else if I were to put blame on anyone. We've seen plenty of people disregarding the government's quarantine and even actively fighting with police over the shutdown of most nonessential businesses. If we are to stop the Virus, we all must do our part. It's as simple as that. Until we can understand how it works and stop the spread or mitigate its effects on those infected, or hopefully both...we all have to make sacrifices for the greater good."

"Right, of course we all have a part to play in this ongoing crisis," the anchorman responded, then continued his questions, "so there are many difficulties in researching this Virus...could you explain what exactly is so challenging about it compared to a more naturally occurring virus?"

"Of course...the difficulty lies in just that. Nothing like this exists in nature, so we have nothing to base our research on...we're starting from scratch. Not to mention that there are several factors that affect how fast and how far a virus can spread. For example we know that the Rodrick Virus has a dormant or asymptomatic state before any signs of infection are shown, but we are still trying to determine how long that period lasts. If we can determine how long a person is an active carrier of the Virus after being infected, that could also help us stop it from spreading farther."

"Is there a rough time frame that you've been able to come up with?" the anchor asked.

"Well a lot of testing is still needed obviously, but our working theory right now is at least two weeks...that's the amount of time between the Times Square attack and the first signs of symptoms appearing in the victims," Dr. Wall answered.

As the anchor continued talking, both with Dr. Wall and about the Virus in general, Jack felt a churning in his stomach as they cut to videos of people who were in the middle of their mutations. The half-formed animal features, bloody bandages, and the moans and screams of pain were almost too much for him. He quickly grabbed the remote and turned the TV off.

Right before he did though, the news cut to an interview with one of the infected people after they had completely changed. It was surreal seeing them sitting calmly in front of the camera and talking as if they hadn't been through a hellish ordeal. The person's new feline features seemed as if they had always been there, and the person themselves seemed to be completely unfazed by their new anatomy, even happy about it.

With the TV now off, Jack could see his pale reflection in the black screen. His expression a mix of disgust and horror. Jack stared at his reflection for a few seconds, lost in thought. He never made a habit of staring at himself in the mirror, but something about seeing those people on the TV and then seeing himself in the screen was unnerving.

He had always told himself that he had never cared about his appearance before, but something about those poor people on the news had made him feel strange about it suddenly. As if he had suddenly realized something that he had been ignoring for a long time. The only problem was that Jack wasn't sure what the thing was, and his mind lingered on the more disturbing images from the news.

Jack stood up from the chair he was sitting in and tried to push the disturbing images and sounds out of his head. He glanced around his meager apartment, the kitchen that doubled as a living room, the small hall that led to his bathroom and the bedroom next to it, and he sighed. Grabbing his thermos full of coffee and his keys, he headed out the door to work.

Jumping into his old truck and turning the key, he was greeted by the radio blaring loudly. He quickly turned the volume down to more acceptable levels for the early morning and checked the clock on the dash. It read quarter past five, which would give him plenty of time to get to work as it was only a ten-minute drive from his apartment. As he drove, he heard the song on the radio suddenly stop and be replaced by the obnoxious blaring of the warning tone that preceded emergency broadcasts. Jack turned the radio up slightly to hear the announcement.

"Attention! This is an emergency broadcast from the CDC concerning the Rodrick Virus," the mechanical sounding voice said flatly.

As it blared, the churning in his stomach was replaced by an uneasy knot. It had been a month since the first stories of the Virus had reached them in their small town of Rawling, Pennsylvania, but it had plenty of people on edge. Even though Rawling had had only a few cases of the Virus since then and almost no cases that went to Stage Two.

Just the thought of it made Jack's stomach turn even worse than before. Being slowly turned into something inhuman was almost too bizarre to believe, like something out of a movie. The broadcast let out a few more warning tones and then the robotic, staticky voice continued.

"The following counties have had multiple cases of both Stage One and Two afflictions appear within the last twenty-four hours: Collin, King, Lucas, Poe, and Reynolds. It is highly advised that individuals living in these areas take strong precautions against the Virus. Including but not limited to wearing a medical grade mask or other face covering at all times, avoiding any individuals who may be experiencing symptoms of the Virus, and staying indoors if possible. The CDC reminds all those who believe they are infected to report to the nearest hospital to avoid unintentional spread of the Virus. The dormant stage of the Virus is believed to last for two weeks, and early symptoms can include dizziness, fever, cough..." the broadcast trailed off as it began listing symptoms of the Virus, but Jack had heard them all before, and he was still in shock at having heard the list of affected counties.

Rawling was in King County, and all the other counties listed either surrounded King or were near it. As he pulled into the parking lot at work, he asked himself why he was still coming to work in the first place. All the schools had been closed for weeks, and by the way things were going, they weren't opening any time soon.

Yet here he was, and as he got out of his truck, he noticed that there was only one other vehicle in the parking lot, his boss's SUV. The garage bay was open, so he walked in looking for his boss, Mary. It didn't take long to find her standing by a supply shelf at the back of the bay.

She saw him and motioned for him to come over. Jack noticed she was wearing a face mask, and as he approached her, she held one out for him. He took it and put it on, but he felt no safer for it. Her short dark hair looked especially frazzled as she pulled the mask slightly away from her mouth to speak more clearly.

"I'm glad you're here, Jack! I thought no one else would show up! But I can't be too hard on the other guys, what with this weird disease going around and everything..."

"It's a virus..." Jack corrected her, "...but yeah, I know what you mean. Although you have to admit, it is kind of ridiculous that we're even here to begin with. I mean school's been closed for weeks, and even the administrators haven't been in to work in a week."

"Yes, but they want the school ready for when they do reopen it. We can't let the work pile up, or we'll have a terrible time tackling it later." She countered, "Besides, there's no arguing with them. We just have to do what we can with what we have."

This was a favorite saying of hers, and it annoyed Jack to no end. However, he conceded that even if he were to go home now, there was a good chance that if any of them were going to be infected, they already were. His boss had a good heart and was always looking out for him and the other guys that worked at the school. And he didn't think he could leave her to do everything by herself anyway, especially if she ended up getting infected. With that thought, he gave his boss a shrug and headed for his mower.

Since the school was closed, he had started just riding out on the mower and cutting whatever grass seemed like it needed it the most. That was just what he did today, too, and he tried not to think about the Virus or that it had finally made its presence fully known in his hometown. However, try as he may, it still hung in the back of his mind all day while he worked.

It wasn't too bad at first, and he was able to just focus on his work. After a few hours, however, Jack heard an ambulance scream down the road near where he was mowing, and a chill ran down his spine. He adjusted his mask and kept mowing.

Then a little while later, while mowing near the edge of the school's property, he heard people arguing loudly. They're voices were muffled partly, and Jack wondered why. Until three people came stumbling awkwardly out the front door of one of the houses that lined the street opposite the area he was mowing.

All three were wearing masks, not unlike the one Jack wore, and two, a middle-aged couple, were leading the third, an elderly man who seemed to be trying to resist them, outside. Now that they were outside, Jack could hear part of what they were saying, but only partially because of the noise from the mower.

"Please, Dad! Don't fight us! –trying to help you!" the woman pleaded with the older man.

"I told you I don't need to go to the hospital!" the old man roared.

"You heard the news. We need – hospital and have you checked! What if – Virus?! –put everyone in danger?! What about the kids?!" the man retorted.

They continued to argue and fight towards the car, but Jack couldn't hear any more of what they were saying. Eventually they got the old man into the car and sped off towards the hospital. Jack sorely wished that was the first and last time he saw such a scene, but it wasn't.

After what seemed like an eternity, it was finally time to go home. Jack rode his mower into the garage bay and parked it in its usual spot. As he was filling the gas tank, Mary walked into the bay.

"How did things go today?" she asked. Jack shrugged in response. "A shrug? That's all I get?!" Mary said, pretending to be annoyed at him. He shrugged again; a smile hidden under his mask. "What am I supposed to do with you?" she said as she rolled her eyes.

Mary always knew how to break the tension in a situation. She had to have heard the sirens and ambulances all day. After all she had been working in the area around their maintenance building, which had more houses around it than anywhere Jack had been working. Everyone was on edge, and it wasn't hard to understand why. Jack talked with Mary while he finished putting things away and getting things ready for the next day.

"So what do we do if things keep getting worse around here?" he asked.

"Well I certainly don't want to put myself or anyone else in danger..." she said, thinking for a moment before responding. "If this whole Virus thing gets any worse, we'll just have to go to the administration and tell them that we won't be in until it's safe."

"You think they'll agree to that?" he responded.

"They'll have to if they want their grass mowed," she said firmly, then added, "don't worry...I don't think anyone's job is in danger right now...I think they're just being stubborn, or they don't realize how dangerous the Virus is. Hopefully that'll change now..."

"Yeah, I guess it will be pretty hard to ignore now, and I don't think things are going to get any better anytime soon ..." he added, agreeing with her, "...but I'm not sure how things could get any worse now that the Virus is actually here in town...."

They both nodded, and Jack finished cleaning up. He clocked out and said goodbye to Mary as he headed out the door. Getting in his truck, Jack felt the all too familiar knot in his stomach tighten.

Things were certainly not going to be getting better, in fact it seemed like things could only get worse from this day on. Jack was worried, not only for his own safety but for his family's safety as well. His parents also lived in Rawling. Although they lived just outside of town, so they were a little safer than he was living in town.

Chapter 2: Stage One

A few days passed with little improvement since the outbreak had reached King County, and Jack had been to work every day since, as was Mary. Despite their agreement, neither one had said anything about not coming in to work in the past few days. But he had decided that today would be the last day he worked until the school reopened and he was determined to convince Mary to do the same. It wouldn't be easy, but he had to at least try, and he didn't think he could call off in good conscience knowing she would be by herself.

He walked into the garage bay around lunchtime to try and talk to Mary about taking off. The ambulances and people being dragged off to the hospital had been even worse than the first day and had been especially bad that morning. She was sitting at the break table in the corner of the bay eating lunch when he came in. Seeing Jack she went to greet him, but he was surprised to see a look of fear come over her as he approached.

"What's wrong?" he asked.

"Your face!" she answered. "It's so pale! Are you feeling alright?"

"Yeah...I feel fine," he said, puzzled. This wasn't the first time Mary had thought someone was sick because of the way they looked, so Jack wasn't immediately concerned.

But she still told him, "Well you just sit here and rest at least."

"Actually I was just going to take my break if that's alright?" Jack said, knowing the answer already.

Mary scowled and motioned for him to sit. There were a lot of things Mary would joke about, being sick was not one of them, and Jack couldn't blame her given the current circumstances. They sat and talked for a while, and Jack managed to somehow convince her to call the administration to insist that they be given some time off.

She told Jack it was likely that they would only agree if they used their own sick time or vacation. He shook his head and agreed that if that was what they had to do, then it would be worth it. Mary agreed, probably more for Jack's sake than hers, as she was still not convinced that he was okay.

Jack got up from his seat as Mary headed to her office, which was an old desk in the opposite corner of the bay, and he headed for his mower to continue working. He only made it a few steps, however, before he was suddenly overcome with dizziness. Stopping suddenly he braced himself against the nearby wall for balance. Mary, seeing him stop suddenly, came rushing over to help. She grabbed his arm and helped him back to his chair. Looking at him with a worried expression, she put a hand to his forehead and quickly took it away.

"Are you okay? You have a fever."

"I don't know..." Jack answered truthfully. "One minute I was fine, and then I just got so dizzy, I thought I was going to fall down."

"Jack...." Mary said quietly. "I don't want you to panic, but you know those are some of the first symptoms, right?"

His stomach dropped at her words. Of course they were, and he hadn't even considered it, even though the news and radio had been listing them all over and over for a month. He tried to stay calm and think of some of the other symptoms, coughing blood, nausea, body aches, disorientation, vomiting. His mind was reeling at the thought that he might be infected. Luckily Mary was levelheaded in situations like this and knew what their next step should be.

"We need to get you to the hospital. You never know, it might not be the Virus?" she said encouragingly. "But we should go now before you get any worse." As she said this, she stood and held out her hands for him, "Do you think you can stand?"

"Yeah…" he answered, taking her hand.

Mary helped Jack to her car, as it was closer and would be easier to get into. His head still swimming, he could hardly think straight as she put his seat belt on for him. He thanked her profusely as she got in and started the car.

"Don't worry about it, Jack, everything's going to be fine," she said the last part to him, but he knew it was more to calm her own nerves.

They drove towards the hospital, and every few minutes Mary would glance over at Jack to see if he was okay, a look of concern on her face. About halfway to the hospital, another symptom manifested when Jack was overcome with a coughing fit. He could taste the irony blood in his mouth before he saw the blood on his mask.

A look of horror came over Mary's face as she saw the blood, and she drove a little faster. Jack's stomach was twisting in knots, but he wasn't sure if it was a symptom or stress from the situation. Either way the ride to the hospital felt like it took hours, but Jack knew it was only twenty minutes or so.

As Mary parked the car and got out to help Jack inside; he had accepted the fact that he was infected, what else could it possibly be? He didn't need a test to see the writing on the wall. The symptoms were too specific, and only someone in denial would think otherwise.

That also meant that he had to face another fact. Most people who showed symptoms were dead within a week or two. And the alternative was considered worse than death by just about everyone who had seen the news stories about it.

He was in a fog as Mary helped him into the hospital and sat him down in the waiting room. His mind was swimming between the dizziness and the thoughts that his life would most likely be over soon. There was so much he wanted to do, so much of life he hadn't experienced. Just as he was struggling with all this, Mary sat down beside him.

"Okay, I got you checked in, and they said someone would be out as soon as possible, but it could be a while; there are a lot of people ahead of us."

She put a hand on his shoulder. Jack looked around and realized the waiting room was full of people. *Of course it was*, he thought, they were in the middle of a pandemic. Mary took out her phone and turned to Jack.

"Do you have your parents' number? I was going to call them for you... if you want..."

"Oh, yeah, just use my phone if it's easier," Jack said, handing her his phone.

She called his parents and explained what was going on, and when she hung up, she told Jack they were on their way. He would have protested, but he knew he was in no shape to argue. As promised his parents showed up a little while later. Jack's mom immediately put a hand on his forehead to check his temperature and asked him a barrage of questions about how he felt and what was wrong. Thankfully he was saved from answering the questions when a nurse came and led him to a room.

They went through the standard procedures, like taking his weight, temperature, and blood pressure. Jack was surprised by how calm and collected the nurse was, even though he knew she and all the other staff had to be going through a lot dealing with the pandemic. Then the first nurse left, promising someone would be in shortly to see him. He wasn't sure how long he sat in that room, it could have been five minutes or five hours. When the doctor finally came in, he smiled, introduced himself, and set a syringe down on the small, stainless-steel table that sat next to the bed Jack sat on.

"Hello! I'm Dr. Hawthorn. Now to test for the Roderick Virus, we need to take a blood sample," he said. "And just so you know, we've had quite a few false alarms today, so there's a good chance it's not that."

Jack was sure he was trying to sound hopeful, but he could see the truth of the situation. After the doctor was done, he took the sample and told Jack it would take about thirty minutes to run the test. When he left, Jack wondered how long it would take before his parents insisted on coming back to his room. As if on que, his phone rang; it was his mom.

"Hey, how are you? They wouldn't let us come back to see you, so I thought I'd call. Did they run any test yet?" she asked.

"Just took blood for the test...doctor said it'd be about thirty minutes," Jack answered.

His head wasn't swimming as badly as before, perhaps sitting still in the quiet room was helping. Waiting was the hardest part, especially when you were waiting for something so dire. So he stayed on the phone with his mom but stayed quiet.

His parents and Mary passed the time by talking. It occurred to Jack that the three of them had never really talked at any great length. They had meet in the past briefly, but this was the first time the three of them had really sat down and had a conversation. Jack was just happy to be left alone, besides, he doubted if he had it in him for idle conversation.

Jack's parents were just as average as Jack was. Both had dark brown hair with a few silver strands poking through, wore glasses, and were of average heights and weights. They were generally friendly to everyone, and his Mom in particular found it easy to strike up a conversation with just about everyone. He sat and listened to her do just that with Mary as his Dad sat beside her and listened to them intently.

After another eternity, Dr. Hawthorn returned holding a folder full of papers. He took one out and sat down solemnly as Jack put his parents and Mary on speaker phone so they could hear. Clearing his throat, the doctor began.

"Hello, everyone," he said, acknowledging Jack's parents and Mary, "I have the test results here and...well...I'm afraid it isn't good news..." he paused, and Jack could tell his mom was holding back tears, even without seeing her. "The test came back positive. Mr. Towzer, I'm afraid you've contracted the Roderick Virus." At these last few words, Jack's mom launched into another barrage of questions, but Dr. Hawthorn stopped her by saying, "Ma'am, I'll be happy to answer all your questions, but first your son needs to be quarantined."

Jack spent the next several minutes changing into a gown a nurse had brought him after he had ended the call with his parents. His parents had promised to return the next day, but he wasn't sure if they would even be allowed to see him since he was quarantined in this little room. He spent the rest of the day mindlessly flipping through channels on the TV, continuing to cough up blood, and despairing at his inevitable fate.

His condition would only get worse over the next two weeks, and it took an entire week before anyone could visit him. Even then they were only allowed to stay for fifteen minutes and had to wear hazmat suits, or at least something that looked like one. Jack wasn't sure if they were actual hazmat suits or if they were something similar.

By the end of the first week, his dizziness had come and gone multiple times. He was now coughing and vomiting blood and was exhibiting all the other symptoms of the Virus as well. Also, he had to be fed intravenously because he couldn't keep anything down.

As the second week ended, Jack knew his time was almost up. And by this time, his body had begun to ache all over, and he felt exhausted all the time. The idea that he was probably only a day or less from death was almost comforting towards the end.

Jack had trouble keeping track of the days as his condition worsened. But the nurses and doctors who would come in to check on him would tell him what day it was and how long he had been in the hospital for. Which was both good and bad.

He was happy that they did it though because it was better to know how much time he had left rather than not. It still surprised him when Dr. Hawthorn came into his room one day and told him that he had good news and bad news. Jack asked for the bad news first.

"Well it's kind of the same news..." Dr. Hawthorn laughed but then continued, becoming somewhat more serious. "What I mean is it's either good news or bad news, depending on how you look at it." Seeing the puzzled look on Jack's face, the doctor smiled and gave him a reassuring look as he said, "Today marks the beginning of the third week since you were admitted to this hospital. Which means the Rodrick Virus isn't going to kill you...you've entered Stage Two."

Chapter 3: Stage Two

For the second time in two weeks, Jack's world was turned upside down. And for the second time in two weeks, Jack sat in stunned silence for a long time. His parents, upon hearing the news, were filled with a mix of relief, fear, and uncertainty but not as much as Jack was.

He, like everyone else, had seen the news stories and he knew exactly what was going to happen to him now. Slowly and painfully he would change. It wasn't known what caused people to enter Stage Two while others died or how exactly Stage Two did what it did. Also, it wasn't known what kind of animal a person would resemble after it was over. Jack couldn't help but run all this over and over in his head as he lay in his hospital bed.

Since hearing the news, Jack had started to feel better, but again he felt like this was just the calm before the storm. Another good thing about entering Stage Two, at least that was how Jack had decided to think of it, was that he was no longer considered contagious. Jack's parents had come to visit him, and now free from the hazmat suits, they were able to stay longer, and he could hear them more clearly when they spoke.

They spent a lot of time asking questions about the Virus and what Stage Two meant, but this was more out of nervousness and concern rather than actually not knowing about it. Like everyone else, they knew what was going to happen, and they knew what the result would be. After the roughly two to three-week process, Jack would be something different, something inhuman. Unexpectedly Jack's dad posed a question Jack hadn't considered yet.

"So...you can't really choose what kind of animal you'll resemble but... do you have any preferences? Maybe one or two you wouldn't mind looking like?"

Both Jack and his mom looked at him like he had just spoken another language, and Jack felt slightly angered by the question. It made it seem like he wanted to change, which he certainly did not. Just the thought of what was going to happen was upsetting enough. Who could possibly, in their right mind, want to become something inhuman, an animal?

"What?" his dad responded. "I just thought that...well...we've been sitting here talking about all the negatives in this situation instead of the positive. And besides, it's a good distraction from everything else. So? Did you have anything in mind, son?"

"Um...I...I don't know...I guess I'd have to think about it?" Jack answered, unsure of how exactly to answer and still somewhat upset by the question in general, even if his dad had meant well by it.

On the one hand, there were plenty of animals that Jack liked, but none that he liked so much he wanted to be one. He was briefly reminded of seeing his reflection in the black TV screen. Jack's dad had brought up a good point though, he had to try and dwell on the positives. That was the only way he would survive his coming ordeal because, like it or not, it was going to happen, and there was nothing he, or anyone, could do to stop it.

Jack listed the positives in his head. First, he wasn't going to die, and second, there would probably be some benefit to being whatever animal he became. Like a dog having a good sense of smell, or a hawk having good eyesight. Unfortunately those were the only two positives Jack could think of at the moment. However, there were also plenty of negatives he had to avoid thinking about. For example how painful the actual transformation would be, or if he became an animal with a huge weakness or fault, like a fish not being able to breath out of water.

He was just about to ask his parents for their thoughts on the matter, but before he could, a nurse knocked on the door. As she entered, she told them that their visiting time had ended.

So Jack gave them a shrug and said, "Well I guess I'll see you tomorrow..."

Jack's parents assured him that they would be in to see him, and they left. The room was quiet as the nurse examined the machines Jack was hooked into. She asked him the same routine questions they asked him every day.

"How do you feel? Any vomiting? Any new symptoms, aches, or pains?" Jack answered all her questions, and she smiled and left with her clipboard in hand.

A little while later, Jack's whole body began to ache, like a mild sunburn all over his body. It wasn't long, however, before it got worse. Over the next few days, Jack's vomiting increased to nearly every hour, and his aches had gone from mild sunburn to the feeling of needles sticking him all over.

As time passed, the pain increased in certain areas, like his head, hands, and legs. His legs were especially painful, and by the third day, it was so painful, he couldn't walk at all. The pain in his head made it hard to think, and he spent hours on end writhing in pain in his bed. It also didn't help that the hospital had denied him from having visitors during this stage of the Virus. Not that he would have wanted anyone to see him in the state he was in or been able to even acknowledge that they were even there.

Jack noticed the first of the physical changes on the fourth day. He had lost all the hair on his head, and his skin had become loose and wrinkled in some places. His stomach felt better on the fifth day, but his legs felt like the bones had been shattered and his muscles had been through a blender. It was on this same day that his headaches subsided, and Jack was able to think clearly for the first time in days.

All he could think about, other than the pain in his legs, was what his dad had asked him the last time he talked to him; what animal did he want to be or think he would end up as? He was sure he just wanted to be himself. All the doctors and nurses had told him they wouldn't be able to tell exactly until he was closer to the end of his transformation. But they could take clues from what was happening to him and make educated guesses and rule out certain animals.

Based on where he was experiencing the most pain, they were able to rule out birds of any kind. They all experienced extreme pain in the head and arms, similar to the pain Jack felt in his legs. Which was common in most of the infected as many animals have very different leg structure compared to humans. That was also where some of the most drastic changes would happen. All the doctors and nurses agreed, however, that it was still a little early to determine anything else.

The physical changes became more drastic as time marched on. By the sixth day, Jack had grown thick, dark pads on his palms and fingertips. His teeth had started to fall out as well, and a thin layer of short, dark hair had begun to grow all over his body.

He would spend the seventh day in such excruciating pain that he lost and regained consciousness several times. And when he was conscious, he could do little but scream and writhe in agony. It was also at this time he became aware that the shape of his face had begun to change as well.

The area around his jaw and nose had begun to stretch out from his face, his nose was becoming flat and wide, and his ears had begun to grow and stretch. It was as if his mouth were trying to escape the confines of his face. Strangely his skin didn't tear or split as one might expect from such a development; instead it seemed to stretch painfully as the newly formed bone in his face grew.

Jack's legs were even worse, as he saw during one of his conscious moments. Long, thin lesions had formed running the length of his legs like large, painful stretch marks. They oozed and bled constantly.

The nurses came in frequently, placing bandages and gauze under and around his legs and changing them as often as possible. Which wasn't very often because they had a difficult time moving him. Given his state, they had to be careful not to cause him even more pain, as any movement would cause shooting, white hot pain to run through his legs.

At one point, late on the seventh day, the nurses went to change his bandages, and he saw as they lifted his legs that they now had an extra joint between his knee and ankle that seemed to bend the wrong way. This of course shocked Jack and caused him to yell out in both surprise and pain. But as strange as it was, the nurses didn't seem surprised in the least.

They even reassured him that it was common for Anthros to have digitigrade legs. Which they then had to explain that digitigrade legs were the type of legs you commonly saw on dogs, horses, and most other four-legged mammals. Animals with these legs walk on their toes, and the joint below the knee was actually the ankle and the lowest joint was part of the foot.

Jack couldn't fully process everything the nurses had told him until the next day when the pain in his legs had subsided to the point where he could think clearly again. He thought about what they had called him, an Anthro. It hadn't really crossed his mind before as he had been too concerned with other things. Now that he was thinking about it, it seemed strange to be called something other than human, and he felt the anger from before return.

He avoided looking at his legs under the blanket that day, for fear of what he might see. One thing he couldn't avoid was the fact that he now had a very prominent snout, which he inspected tentatively with his hands. They also felt strange thanks to the pads that had formed on them.

Jack lifted his lip on one side of his new snout and felt his new teeth poking through his gums. They were sharp, especially his canines. In addition to these changes, he also took stock of his new hair, or was it fur? It covered him from head to toe and was mostly a dark grey with some parts being a lighter grey, white, and brown and was also very fine and short.

The pain in his hands, which had subsided during the eighth day, returned with a vengeance on the ninth, as did the pain in his legs, specifically in his feet and lower legs. This pain would remain for the tenth day as well. It was also on this day that Jack would begin to feel a sharp, stabbing pain in his lower back. He realized, to his horror, that he had begun to grow a tail.

It was also on the tenth day that the doctor informed Jack that they had narrowed down what he was becoming. Which was some kind of canine or possibly a bear but most likely a dog, wolf, or fox. This was based on the color of his fur and the shape of his snout and ears.

Jack didn't know whether to be happy or upset that they had narrowed it down. Mostly because he was still unsure of how he would be able to function as an Anthro. The more he learned about what was happening to him and the more his body changed, the angrier and more irritable he became.

By the eleventh day, all Jack's teeth had come in, and he learned that the pain in his hands was due to the black claw-like nails that were growing on the end of each finger, which replaced his normal fingernails. After talking with the nurses and doctor, he learned that his voice had dropped in pitch slightly, becoming deeper and slightly more gravely. His fur continued to grow in as well, becoming thicker and longer as it did. The pain in his back had gotten worse, and he was no longer able to lie in bed normally. This also made it more painful for his feet, which continued to send shooting pains up his legs.

On the twelfth day, Jack finally worked up the courage to look at his legs, as the pain had finally subsided. As he took the blanket off, his breath caught in his throat. His legs were, in fact, digitigrade. His thighs had become shortened, and his legs now had three joints instead of two, but perhaps what was most surprising were his feet.

Both were large, larger than he could have ever imagined, and looked almost exactly like a dog's, complete with short, stubby toes ending in black claws and pads on the soles of his feet. Jack was happy to see that the lesions had almost completely healed as well. But the new changes to his body did little to help his worsening mood.

The thirteenth day felt like a repeat of the seventh, as Jack was once again in excruciating pain. His tail was now fully grown and wasn't quite as painful as it had been, but since he wasn't yet used to having a tail, it still made laying on his back uncomfortable. Worse yet was the searing, burning pain that seemed to envelope his entire body. It felt like every nerve in his body had been set on fire.

It came in waves, and each one was worse than the last. All Jack could do was lay in his hospital bed and pray the pain would subside. Any movement, even yelling out in pain, caused it to become even worse. A fact that Jack found unbelievable as the pain was already unbearable. But there was nothing else for him to do but endure it.

And endure it he did. All through that day and the next. It felt like an eternity to Jack, but he knew it was only two days because he hadn't slept at all and had seen the sun move across the sky. Strangely, despite the pain, Jack had remained conscious throughout the ordeal. He didn't know why, but he guessed it had something to do with the amount of adrenaline in his system, at least he thought he had heard something like that once.

Finally, on the fifteenth day of his transformation, all the pain subsided but was replaced with a paralyzing numbness. Jack lay in his bed for the entire day, totally unable to move, even a little. This did, however, give Jack time to think. A million thoughts raced through his brain, one after another in quick succession. Everything from "How am I going to walk?" to "What are my parents going to say when they see me?"

His mind was also overcome with a mix of anger, sadness, confusion, and despair. With his change almost complete, there was no getting around it anymore. He had become an animal, a monster, something inhuman. And he felt his whole body fill with the searing anger that had been slowly building within him since he entered Stage Two.

Why him?

What did he do to deserve such a fate?

How could he live like this?

He had lived when so many others hadn't and knew that he should be grateful, but he couldn't help but think that maybe they had been the lucky ones?

This barrage of questions and thoughts were interrupted by a knock on the door. Jack tried to turn his head to see who it was but was still not able to move. As they approached the bed, he saw that it was the doctor, Hawthorn. He smiled at Jack and sat down beside the bed.

"Well! Look who's finally through the worst of it!" he said warmly. "You know, you took it like a champ. You really did. Most scream for days on end, especially towards the end..." his smile faded for a second, then returned. "But you probably have questions. So I thought I'd pop in and see if I couldn't answer a few. Now you obviously can't move right now, don't worry, that's normal, but I have a list of frequently asked questions that I'll just go over."

Dr. Hawthorn smiled again, then shuffled through a small stack of papers he had brought with him. Jack knew that the doctor was only trying to help and give him as much information as possible. Yet he couldn't help but feel annoyed and upset by his almost constant upbeat attitude. To him it felt like the doctor was almost making light of the horrible situation Jack found himself in, even though he knew that wasn't the case. Lifting one of the pages out of the stack, the doctor cleared his throat and began to speak.

"Now first things first, you're probably wondering what kind of animal you resemble. Maybe you already figured this out, but just in case you haven't, I'll tell you that, in your case, you're a wolf, specifically a Timber Wolf."

Jack had thought he started to resemble a dog of some kind, and the doctor had said as much before, but a wolf?! It was such a strange feeling. He guessed he should be happy he ended up as something close to normal as opposed to something weird, like an angler fish or something. But all he felt was anger and the strange feeling from before. The only difference now was that he had a face to put with it, so to speak.

"Now..." Dr. Hawthorn continued, "as far as your loved ones are concerned, they will be informed of your progress and will be able to visit you tomorrow once you're able to move again. And I'm sure they'll be excited to see you, so try not to worry about it too much, okay? I know the thought of seeing your loved ones after what you've been through must be difficult to process. You're probably worrying about what they'll think, but it will be fine, trust me."

Jack knew Hawthorn was just trying to be nice and reassure him that everything was going to be okay, but it didn't help him at all. He knew he should trust the doctor, after all he had to have seen dozens of Anthros since the Virus first appeared, if not more. So if anyone could guess what someone's reaction to seeing their son as one for the first time would be, it would probably be him. However, Jack was still going to worry about it, and he knew there would be little he or anyone could do about it.

"Finally," the doctor added, "you're probably wondering how much longer you'll be here? Well I'm afraid it's going to depend on how quickly you learn to walk again. As you already saw, your legs are now what is called digitigrade, and that is going to take some getting used to. So you'll start physical therapy tomorrow, and with any luck, you'll be walking unassisted in a week or so. You'll be amazed at how quickly your body will adapt." And with that, Hawthorn smiled again and got up from his chair and left the room, promising to check on him again tomorrow morning.

The next morning, Dr. Hawthorn returned as promised. Reaching into his lab coat, he pulled out a small hand mirror. He handed it to Jack, who had indeed regained his ability to move.

Jack took the mirror, and the doctor explained, "You haven't seen yourself yet, have you? Well here. Have a look for yourself." And seeing Jack's reluctance to look, he added, "Whenever you're ready of course. This isn't exactly the kind of thing you want an audience for, so I'll leave you to it." And just as abruptly as he had entered, Hawthorn left, and Jack was left alone with the mirror.

Jack carefully turned the mirror upwards, towards the ceiling. He wasn't sure why, but he was scared. That strange feeling from before was back as well and stronger than ever. Knowing what he probably looked like didn't help his fear either. It was one thing to be told you look like something and an entirely different thing to see it for yourself. Still, as he lifted the mirror towards his face, his hand started to tremble.

Why was he so scared?

He had already seen the rest of his new body, why fear this?

Was it because if he saw his face, there would be no denying what he had become?

That he was no longer human?

That he was an animal?

A monster?

Jack steadied his hand and lifted the mirror higher.

"Have to face the facts one day anyway," Jack told himself, "might as well be today..."

He lifted the mirror fully to his face. It took everything he had to stop himself from letting out a scream of pure horror. Jack's face was, in fact, a wolf's. To be exact, his entire head looked like a wolf's, as if someone had taken a wolf's head and sewn it onto his body.

After taking a few minutes to catch his breath and collect himself, Jack examined his new face more closely. He remembered his ears starting to grow and become pointed but hadn't realized that they had also migrated further up, now sitting almost on top of his head. His eyes had also changed without him realizing it. From their original brown color to a piercing yellow.

Jack stared into his new eyes for a long time, and he could feel the strange feeling inside him growing stronger as he stared. He wasn't sure why, but he felt better, having seen them. Maybe it was the distinctive color they had become, compared to the boring brown they had been. Or maybe it was that he could still see himself in them, could still see what made him, him in them. Either way Jack felt just a little better about himself and his predicament, at least for a short while anyway.

Chapter 4: An Offer

A short while later, after Jack had finished examining his new face with the mirror, there came a knock on the door. It was a nurse, and she announced that Jack's parents had arrived to see him. Jack's heart jumped to his throat. What would they say? What would they think? Would they even believe he was their son? All these questions and a thousand more shot through his head as the door slowly opened.

Thinking quickly Jack threw the blanket over his head to hide his appearance, at least initially, from them. He hoped it would be less of a shock that way, although he felt silly sitting in the bed with a blanket over his head. Jack could see through the thin blanket and watched them enter the room. His mom looked nervously at the nurse, but she bid her forward reassuringly.

"J-Jack?" she asked nervously. "Is that you, sweetie?" She took a few steps closer, then looked back at the nurse, who motioned for her to get closer.

"Y-Yeah...it's me," Jack stammered back, and he winced as the sound of his voice made his parents flinch. He had forgotten that his voice had changed as well.

"Can we see you, sweetie?" his mom asked tentatively. "Dr. Hawthorn told us you looked like a wolf, so we wouldn't be surprised when we see you. I know that you're worried we might think differently about you now, but you're still our son, and we love you no matter what you look like."

Jack could feel a mix of anger and sadness welling up inside him, tears as well, but he held them back. He sat still, keeping the blanket over his head but turning more towards his parents. His mom stepped back slightly, his dad right behind her, then they both took a few more steps closer to the bed. They were staring at Jack through the blanket, and he wanted to pull it off himself but just didn't have it in him.

As if realizing this, his mom said tentatively, "Okay, Jack. I'm going to pull off the blanket now."

She reached out and took hold of the blanket. Gently pulling it off him, slowly revealing his new features, his ears, snout, eyes, fur, everything was now in the open. Jack blinked, looking at both his parents.

Before anyone could say anything, his mom wrapped her arms around him in a hug and said, "Jack! Oh, it's so good to see you again! We were so worried!" He was surprised by her sudden embrace but gladly wrapped his arms around her in return. His dad stepped forward, breaking his silence since they entered the room.

"Alright, alright, give the boy some space," he said in his usual, jovial tone. "Can't you see you're embarrassing him in front of the pretty nurse."

Jack's dad nudged him in the shoulder and winked. If it weren't for his fur, everyone would have seen Jack's face turn bright red. Though he was glad his parents were still acting as they always did.

He would spend the better part of the day talking with his parents and telling them about his new body. For the first time, Jack was able to think about something other than how terrible what had happened was, and he was able to push all the negative feelings and emotions to the back of his mind, if only temporarily. Late in the day, Dr. Hawthorn returned with two nurses and informed them that it was time for Jack's physical therapy.

The two nurses carefully helped Jack stand, and he took his first, shaky step. His new feet made it difficult to stand and his new legs made it hard to balance. Resulting in Jack falling several times just trying to take a single step.

For over an hour the nurses and Hawthorn helped Jack try and walk. Unfortunately, in that time, he had only managed to walk the length of the room once, and with a great deal of difficulty and help from the nurses. Still the doctor reassured him that he would get the hang of it in no time and before long he'd be walking as well as he had before his transformation.

Dr. Hawthorn and the nurses would return and help Jack walk more and more and with less assistance every day. By the end of the week, he was walking the full length of the hallway outside his room with no trouble. It was after one such walk that Jack was told he had a special visitor. Curious as to who it could be, he sat patiently in his room while the nurse led the visitor inside.

Jack's parents wouldn't be in until later that day, as they had been coming to visit him every day that week after work. Mary, although she had not come to visit him, had been keeping in touch through his parents. He wasn't all that close to any of the other people he worked with, so that ruled out anyone Jack could think of who would have come to visit him. So he reasoned it had to be a stranger, but what they wanted with him, he couldn't begin to guess.

His questions would be answered when the nurse returned a short while later with the visitor in question. The man was short, portly, and an Anthro who resembled a pig. Much like Jack, the visitor's head and legs were similar to the animal he resembled. The Anthro was also covered in a course but thin, white hair, and his pink skin was clearly visible through it.

At the sight of him, Jack's anger, which he had been able to keep mostly at bay the last few days, came raging back. It was as if seeing another Anthro had reminded Jack of what he was now, something inhuman. The pig Anthro wore a neat blue suit and tie and carried himself with an air of self-importance, as if he was someone of great authority.

This only further infuriated Jack as he couldn't stand those kinds of people. Entering the room, he approached Jack and held out his hand. Jack shook it, not wanting to seem rude, and the Anthro smiled and introduced himself.

"Hello! Young man...you must be Jack Towzer, very happy to meet you!" he spoke with the same self-importance and slurred his words slightly, as if he were talking with his mouth half full. "My name is Jason Buchannon, and I represent the Anthro community of Claw Creek. We're looking for fine, upstanding citizens to join our community, and you, my boy, are just the sort of people we want!" his jowls shook as he talked.

He couldn't quite put his finger on it, but there was something about Buchannon that he didn't like. Besides his self-important, pompous air and the fact that he seemed proud to be an animal. Buchannon reminded Jack of a stereotypical sleazy salesman more than anything. Jack found himself staring at his jowls as he talked.

"Now I know you've got questions, so ask away!" Buchannon continued.

"You represent an Anthro community?" Jack asked, genuinely curious but still annoyed.

"Yes, indeed! One of what I'm sure will be many!" Buchannon answered.

"And this community is only for Anthros?" Jack asked, continuing to question Buchannon's motives.

"Well...not entirely. If you have any family that aren't Anthro, they're more than welcome," Buchannon added. "In fact we have several younger Anthros that move there with their human parents, or brothers, or sisters..." he trailed off, and Jack flinched at the word "human." Another reminder of what he was now.

"I see...so can you tell me a bit more about this community? Where is it? How big is it? Things like that?" Jack continued his questions, trying not to sound angry or annoyed.

"Of course! Well, to start, Claw Creek is located about fifteen miles to the southwest of here, and although it's growing bigger and better every day, currently the town is about one square mile and has a population of about 200. The town is also surrounded on every side by fertile farmland, much of which will eventually go towards feeding the town. In fact the whole point of Claw Creek is to create a self-sufficient community by Anthros, for Anthros."

As Buchannon finished his speech, he smiled proudly and gripped the opening of his suit jacket. Jack, however, didn't buy into the whole "self-sufficient, by Anthros, for Anthros" line. He wasn't comfortable with being an Anthro himself, how could he ever live in a community full of them?

Asking another series of questions to humor Buchannon, Jack continued, "So, what exactly would I do in this community? Would I even be able to find a job in such a small town? What about schools? I want to have kids someday, is there a school for them to go to? And what about amenities? Are there stores? A supermarket?"

Buchannon seemed a little surprised by Jack's questions, which Jack had ready because he had thought about all of them whenever he looked at farms that were for sale, but the pig Anthro smiled again and answered, "Of course, of course! No need to worry, my boy!" He laughed and put a hand on Jack's shoulder, further aggravating Jack, "Claw Creek has a school, a small one, but there are already plans for expanding it when the time comes, and there's a supermarket and even a farmer's market in the works. There's also plenty of other establishments, places to buy whatever you need, and all owned and operated by our fellow Anthros. As far as a job, well, you have two choices; we can give you a job doing what you're doing now, except you'd be working for your fellow Anthros instead of humans. Or, if you'd rather, we could find you a job doing something you've always wanted to do...just one of the benefits of getting in on the ground floor!"

Buchannon laughed again and shook Jack's shoulder. Jack was still skeptical, and Buchannon's continued mentioning of humans and Anthros was really starting to get to Jack.

So much so that he was barely able to keep the anger out of his voice, but he was intrigued by the idea of doing something he always wanted to do, so he asked, "So...if I wanted to, say, be a farmer? You'd help me buy a farm? As in help me get it financed or something?"

Buchannon's face spread into a wide smile as he answered Jack's question, "Help you?! Why, my boy, we'd finance it for you! And sell the farm to you at a steeply discounted price. In fact I'm sure we could even get you approved for a loan at the Claw Creek Bank for any startup cost you might have as well."

Jack was certainly interested now but was still cautious as he had always heard if something was too good to be true, it usually was, so he asked, "So...what would the community get in return for helping me? I mean I can't really expect you to do all this and expect nothing in return?"

"Ah, well..." Buchannon said, his tone becoming somewhat less excited, "all we, as a community, would ask is that you put back into the community. For example, if you grow corn, we ask that you sell it to local businesses and residents. Seems only fair, right?"

Yes, it did; after all Jack couldn't see anything wrong with Buchannon's explanation, but it seemed like he was hiding something. Jack still had a bad feeling about this whole thing. It was as if his gut was telling him something felt off, and not just because Buchannon was an Anthro. So not wanting to be rude, Jack told Buchannon, "Well it sounds like a tempting offer, but I'll have to think it over."

"Of course, yes, take all the time you need. I know you'll make the right decision," Buchannon said, finally releasing Jack's shoulder from his grip. He reached into his breast pocket with his stubby, fat fingers. Jack noticed they ended in very thick nails that reminded him of hooves somewhat and pulled out a business card. Handing it to Jack, he said, "Here's my card. When you've decided to join Claw Creek, you give me a call, and I'll personally see to it that we get you set up!" He laughed again, shook Jack's hand vigorously, and said, "Well it was nice talking to you, and I can't wait to hear from you, Jack." With that Buchannon left the room.

Jack was left wondering if the strange feeling was all in his head or if there was something more to Buchannon and Claw Creek than he was letting on. Fortunately Jack didn't have much time to dwell on it, as Dr. Hawthorn walked in not too long after Buchannon left. He seemed in an exceptionally good mood as he informed Jack of his swift recovery. If he continued to show such wonderful improvement, he could be discharged from the hospital in two or three days.

Dr. Hawthorn also gave him a list of things he could learn to do on his own after he was discharged. Jack looked over the list while the doctor talked. He was surprised that they would let him go without helping him learn more. Over the past few days, all he had really focused on learning was walking. And a few other very important things, like how to drink and eat solid foods with his new mouth.

Jack thought, maybe they figured he could learn anything else on his own? Not to mention the hospital was still swamped with patients, so they probably needed the room he was in. Still the list included things he felt were essential, like how to properly clean his fur, since it was thick and unlike normal hair. Or drive a car, although the last point had a note stating that practicing driving should be treated as if he were a new driver learning for the first time since he basically was with his new body.

However, he would have to take it easy for another week or two after he left the hospital, and he would have to talk to his employer about when he could return to work. The thought of returning to work made his stomach churn, as he hadn't even thought about it since being admitted to the hospital. Jack resolved to call Mary once he was released to see about work, and he took comfort in knowing that she would be understanding, at least he hoped she would be.

Chapter 5: New Normal

Just as Dr. Hawthorn promised, in three days' time, Jack was discharged from the hospital and sent home. His parents picked him up at noon and drove him to his apartment, despite his mom's protests that he should stay with them for at least a few days. Jack was adamant that he didn't need any help and would be fine on his own. After all he had been walking fine on his own for the last two days he was in the hospital.

Of course his parents still insisted on helping him up the stairs and into his apartment. His mom also insisted on stocking his cabinets and refrigerator with food and making sure he had plenty of other essentials as well. Jack tried to tell them that he would be fine and that he could just go to the store and buy whatever he needed, but they still insisted.

After doing all this, it was finally time for them to leave, and Jack waved them out the door. Even as his mom tried to find a reason to stay. Thankfully his dad was able to convince her to leave by telling her that they would be back tomorrow to check on him and that if he needed anything, he could call.

Once they had left, Jack went to his bedroom and opened the closet. Jack pulled out a pair of his pants, and just as he had expected, it had been altered. All his pants had been altered to include a hole about an inch below the waistline in the back, which allowed his tail to poke through.

Also, every pair of pants had the legs changed to better fit the shape of his new legs. Since his mom had given him an altered pair in the hospital to wear, he had suspected that she had also altered the rest. Although it seemed small, it would be one of the many things that had changed for him.

He stared at the open closet, feeling the anger he had suppressed for the last few days bubbling to the surface. Finally, unable to contain it any longer and no longer under the watchful eyes of the hospital staff, he snapped. Jack began angerly tearing the various clothes out of his closet. Hot tears rolling down his snarling face as he did so.

Why had this happened to him?! What did he do to deserve this?! It wasn't fair!

After the closet stood bare, all the clothes thrown about his room, Jack stood still. His breath was ragged and sounded more like a dog panting than a person. This only angered him more, and he turned towards a mirror, which hung on the wall next to the closet.

He was nothing but an animal now. An inhuman monster. In that moment, he hated everything. The Virus, the man who created it, the school that insisted he work during the outbreak, Dr. Hawthorn, and the nurses who acted so calmly about everything, his parents who seemed to take it all in stride. But more than anything else, he hated himself.

Staring now at his own snarling face did nothing to help. His ears were flat against his head, his eyes wide and wild, his fur covered chest heaved in and out with every breath. Jack approached the mirror, never taking his eyes off his reflection. It was almost unbelievable what he had become, the animal in front of him. The strange feeling he had felt before resurfaced again, stronger than ever before, swelling inside him it felt like his whole body might burst from the pressure. He placed a hand on the mirror and felt the anger swell in his chest as he looked at his hair covered, black-clawed hand.

Jack slammed his hand against the mirror, smashing it. He stared at his now fractured reflection. The anger in his chest turned to sorrow as he did so. It was too much for him to bare, and he raised his head to let out a cry of anguish. To his horror, however, what came out of his mouth was a haunting, mournful howl.

Surprised, Jack quickly grabbed his muzzle. The sorrow he had felt now doubled as he realized that he had been changed not just physically but emotionally as well. He wasn't even able to cry out like a normal human anymore. Even that had been taken from him. Now depressed more than ever, he collapsed onto his bed amidst the clothes and lay there until the next morning, unable to sleep at all that night.

He lay in his bed, staring at his old work boots sitting in the corner as the sunlight pierced the window. Another example of something that had changed. Boots or shoes of any kind would not fit his strangely shaped and oversized feet. This was something he hadn't really noticed in the hospital, but now it was obvious. Still the pads on his feet made things a little easier in that respect as it felt sort of like he was wearing sandals all the time.

As he dragged himself out of bed and began picking up his clothes, he remembered what his dad had said about finding the positives. Clothes didn't make him feel itchy or irritate his fur too badly, he thought. Which was probably because his clothes were all slightly oversized and baggy before he changed.

Jack's clothes weren't the only thing that would be different, however, as he quickly learned when he went to eat breakfast. He had poured himself a bowl of cereal, yet as he lifted the first spoonful to his mouth, he found his new mouth and teeth made it difficult for him to eat as he normally would. The spoon would catch on his large teeth, or he wouldn't place the spoon far enough into his mouth, each time spilling cereal and milk down his front.

He didn't want a repeat of the previous night. So trying to stay as positive as he could, with a sigh, he kept trying. After a few more tries, he finally got the hang of it, even if he did feel ridiculous spilling cereal all over himself. When he was done, he cleaned up his mess and headed to the bathroom for a shower.

This was another new experience for him as an Anthro. His fur became heavy as it got wet, and Jack found it was difficult to move thanks to the weight of his wet fur. He now understood why so many dogs hated baths. Just like with the cereal, however, he persevered. Finally he was able to successfully shower using the special soap Dr. Hawthorn had given him to keep his fur healthy and clean.

Of course drying himself off after his shower proved just as difficult, and Jack resolved to get a hair dryer the next time he went shopping. He then called Mary and explained everything the doctor had said. She asked to come visit him after she got done working, which he begrudgingly agreed to. Mary had apparently only taken off a few days and had gone back to work while he was still in the hospital. The administration had made several of the other maintenance guys come back as well, so she wouldn't be working alone.

Jack spent most of the day tidying up his apartment in preparation for Mary's visit. After all he didn't want his boss to think he was a slob. Later that afternoon, she knocked on the door of the apartment, and Jack answered. He was somewhat nervous as she had only been told about Jack's new appearance and hadn't seen it for herself. Taking a deep breath, he opened the door.

"H-Hello...Mary, come in!" he stammered.

He opened the door as wide as it would go and stepped to one side to allow her to come inside. However, she didn't move after he opened the door. She stood in the hall and stared at him, a confusing look of both shock and awe on her face. Suddenly noticing that she was staring, she quickly shook her head and apologized.

"Sorry, I didn't mean to stare! It's just that I—well..." she seemed at a loss for words.

Jack understood what she meant though. She hadn't been staring on purpose, it was just that she had never seen anything like him before. Jack knew that, had their roles been reversed, he would have stared, too. Anyone would. The emotions from the previous night came flooding back, but he was able to keep his composure. Mary apologized again as he showed her to the kitchen table where they could sit and talk.

"So first things first, I wanted to know how you're doing? Your mom and dad kept me informed while you were in the hospital, but I just wanted to see how you were adjusting. I mean it's a big change, right? So how are you?" Mary asked, nervously glancing around the room, trying to avoid accidentally staring again.

"Well honestly it's been...odd I guess? I mean I've had a few problems here and there but nothing major. So I can't really complain, although it is annoying having to be cooped up here for the next week or so. Plus I'll have to take a driving test again, but that shouldn't be too hard to pass I hope," Jack answered

Jack tried not to let on how he really felt about his situation, as he didn't want Mary or his parents to worry about him. He had scheduled the test for the end of the week, which was the same day as his check up at the hospital. It had been his hope to get the okay to return to work and get his license back all on the same day.

"Oh, well that's good. I'm glad to hear that you're taking everything in stride," Mary said, and Jack had to keep himself from flinching at her words. "So I also came to talk to you about work, you see the administration wants you to come back as soon as possible but also wants to make sure you can still preform all your duties. I have a list here they wanted me to go over with you." She looked at him, then his hands, and asked, "Would you like me to just read the questions to you? Or do you want to fill out the form yourself?" She then took out a sheet of paper from her bag.

"You can read it to me...if you don't mind? I'm not sure how good my handwriting is yet. I haven't really had the chance to practice yet," Jack answered honestly, and Mary nodded, clearing her throat, she began.

"With your new condition, are you still able to operate any and all pertinent equipment?"

"If I can still drive a truck, I think I can run a mower," Jack answered.

"Okay, are you still able to perform general maintenance and care of the various pieces of equipment you use?"

"Yes."

"Are you still able to perform general trimming and weeding duties when needed?"

"Yes."

"Are you still capable of performing general maintenance and repairs around the district?"

"Yes."

"Are you still able to clearly communicate with your superiors and coworkers?"

"I'm talking to you just fine, right?"

"Yes, I know. Sorry, I wasn't the one who wrote up the questions..." Mary apologized. "And finally does your condition impair you in any way from completing any of your duties in a timely and efficient manner?"

"How am I supposed to answer that?" Jack asked, slightly annoyed. "I won't know how long anything will take until I do it at least once."

"I'm sorry, Jack..." she apologized again, "...but I think they just want to make sure it doesn't take you an hour to do a twenty-minute job. You know how picky they can be about efficiency."

"I know..." Jack agreed.

"I'll just put you down as 'to be determined' for that one." She smiled as she wrote it down.

With the paperwork out of the way, they sat and talked about what had happened while Jack had been in the hospital. Mary filled him in on all the things he had missed at work. Which was next to nothing, since it was still closed, and she had only been in a few times for things that were deemed an emergency. Jack, in turn, gave her more details about his time in the hospital and answered any questions she had. After they had been talking for a while, Mary suddenly jumped up.

"Oh my! Is it really that late already?! I'm sorry, Jack, but I have to go! I hadn't planned on being here this long!" Jack assured her that he understood and apologized for keeping her so long.

She hurried out the door and down the stairs of his apartment building, still apologizing as she went. He shut the door to his apartment and went back to his bedroom, where the smashed mirror still hung on the wall. Looking at himself in it, he wondered how strange and frightening he must look to the average person. After all he didn't have to look at himself, and no one had really seen anything like him before, at least not in this small town.

Jack's thoughts turned back to Buchannon's offer. What would it be like to live among other Antros? Would he fit in? Would he stand out? Would anything change at all?

On top of all those questions, Jack still had a weird feeling about the offer and Buchannon. Ultimately he decided to wait and see how things went at work before he decided about Claw Creek. But he couldn't really see himself taking the offer as things were now.

Jack decided, reluctantly, to go out and pick up a few things from the store. Not that he needed much since his parents had stocked up on everything. But he still needed a few other things, like a hair dryer. So Jack grabbed his keys and headed out to the convenience store down the block from his apartment.

As soon as he stepped out of his apartment, Jack was gripped by fear. It suddenly occurred to him that this would be the first time he had been in public since going to the hospital. He had, of course, been in public with his parents after leaving the hospital.

However, they had gone straight to his apartment and now he was by himself. Jack took a deep breath and forced his legs to move. Taking a step towards the exit of the building, he nearly tripped but caught himself.

Jack went down the stairs slowly, being careful not to slip or lose his balance. After making it to the bottom, he opened the door to the building and stepped into the bright sunlight. Turning in the direction of the store, he began walking down the street. He couldn't help but notice the people who were outside stopping and staring.

His chest felt like someone was standing on it. Several times he had to stop himself from turning around and returning to his apartment. He tried to ignore the people on the street, but a few of them were even pointing. He heard a woman gasp from across the street at one point. A car even swerved as the driver stared at him.

It occurred to Jack that maybe everyone hadn't seen all the news broadcasts or heard the radio announcements. But he would have thought that most would have at least some idea of what Anthros looked like. He also considered that, even having known about them, it was entirely different seeing one in person. However, he also knew that some people just had no manners and would stare and point at anyone who was different from them.

Still all the stares made him feel uncomfortable. He was used to being the kind of person who blended into the background and was ignored by others. Jack pressed onwards, and after what felt like an eternity, he made it to the store.

But his problems didn't stop there; as he entered the store, the cashier behind the counter turned and looked at him. The look on her face was a mix of shock and horror. Which Jack couldn't blame her, for as like most of the people on the street, she hadn't seen an Anthro before. As he took a few more steps into the store, however, she stopped him.

"Excuse me! Sir?!" she said the last word as more of a question, as if she wasn't sure what to call him. "You can't come in here like that!" Her voice took on an air of attitude and a hint of anger, "You have to leave!"

"I'm sorry but...what do you mean?" Jack asked, trying to sound as non-threatening and polite as possible but simultaneously feeling like his chest was ready to burst. "Why can't I come in?"

"Ahem..." she cleared her throat and pointed at a sign on the wall by the door that read: No shirt, no shoes, no service. "You're not wearing any shoes!" Her tone sounded like it was the most obvious thing in the world and was full of contempt.

"I'm sorry, ma'am..." Jack explained, trying to keep his voice calm despite her attitude, "But I'm an Anthro. I can't wear shoes."

He lifted one foot up a little so she could see it, but she fired back, "What do I look like?! An idiot?! Of course you're a freak?! You think I care?! The sign says no shoes, no service! So that means GET OUT!"

She yelled the last two words loud enough that it echoed in the small store. Jack was taken aback by her sudden yelling, and he turned around. He ran out of the store with his tail between his legs, both metaphorically and physically.

Jack berated himself for not standing up for himself as he walked further down the street. As well as cursing his situation and blaming everything he could think of. Luckily Jack remembered that there was another store not too far from where he was. And he hoped they would be more accommodating. He hadn't expected to face such hostility, especially in his hometown.

As he walked further down the street, he was met with even more stares, and he swore he could even feel people staring at him from behind. Feeling their eyes burning into him as he walked. He kept his head down, focusing on walking and trying to calm his nerves and temper. Before too long, he found himself at his destination. The small store was tucked back away from the road and had a large parking lot for such a small store.

Jack was concerned with whether they would let him in or not, like the last store. If they wouldn't, he would have to turn back and give up as the next nearest store was too far away to walk. Even if it wasn't, he didn't think he had it in him to go to a third store.

Before he could enter the store, he noticed a woman and a little boy leaving it. Since there was only one small door in and out, he stood to the side to let them exit. Jack also noticed the look of sheer terror on the mother's face as she saw him. Thinking quickly he opened the door for her and tried to smile in a way that didn't seem threatening or frightening. But it wasn't easy because of his large, sharp teeth.

The woman quickly walked through the open door, gripping her son close to her and ignoring Jack completely. Her son stared at him as they passed, his eyes wide in a mix of awe and curiosity. She didn't stop or slow down as she marched the boy straight to their car and quickly got in and left. Jack shrugged his shoulders and sighed; at least they weren't mean or rude to him, but he wasn't sure if being afraid of him was any better.

He walked into the store and looked around, seeing a young woman stood behind the counter at the cash register. She turned to look at him as a small bell on the door announced his arrival as it shut behind him.

She smiled at him and said, "Hello! Is there something I can help you with?"

"Um...yeah, I was looking for a hair dryer?" Jack asked, unsure if the woman would throw him out if she saw he wasn't wearing shoes.

Thankfully she didn't. Instead she helped him find everything he was looking for, including the hair dryer. Jack was so surprised by her kindness that as they made their way to the cash register, he had to ask her.

"Uh, I'm sorry to ask this but..." He hesitated, not wanting to push his luck, but he couldn't help but continue. "Aren't you surprised or scared of me? I mean, I'm an Anthro…there aren't many around here, and everyone else I've met today seems to be either terrified of me or at least shocked by my appearance." If he wasn't covered in fur, the cashier might have noticed that his face was beet red with embarrassment at his own awkward question. The woman just smiled and laughed.

"Yeah, well, I guess they don't see Anthros on a daily basis like me. After all my sister is an Anthro, too. She just got out of the hospital last week."

"Oh, wow…I'm sorry for asking such a stupid question," Jack apologized, now feeling even more embarrassed but surprised by her answer.

"Oh, don't apologize!" she laughed again. "You didn't know, and I've seen the way a lot of people treat Anthros, and it makes me really mad. I mean you'd think they would understand that Anthros are people just like them!" she practically shouted the last sentence but quickly apologized. "Sorry…I didn't mean to raise my voice!"

She quickly rang up the hair dryer and other small items, and Jack paid for them. But before he could leave, she stopped him, "Hey, I don't mean to be nosey, but when you were in the hospital, did you have a guy come and talk to you about a community? Like trying to get you to move there?"

"Yes, actually, his name was Jason Buchannon. Why?" Jack answered.

"That's the same guy that talked to my sister!" she exclaimed. "Did he give you a weird vibe, too? Like something was off about what he was saying?"

"Yeah, I did get that feeling. You did, too?" he asked, not wanting to hint that he had disliked Buchannon for more than his sales pitch.

"I did, but my sister didn't believe me. So now I can tell her that I wasn't the only one who thought he was off." She seemed relieved, and Jack felt a little better about not accepting Buchannon's offer right away, too. "Oh, I'm sorry, I didn't introduce myself. I'm Heather, and my sister's name is Barbara; she's a bat, by the way, but not a vampire bat. She's actually a Flying Fox, a kind of fruit bat." Heather seemed to add the last details as if they were an afterthought.

"Oh, well, it's nice to meet you, Heather, my name's Jack, and as I'm sure you already noticed, I'm a wolf," Jack said, feeling stupid for even adding the last part, but Heather responded, "Oh okay, I thought you might be, but I didn't want to assume…" She smiled again and handed him his bags. Jack smiled back, and as he headed out of the store, she called after him, "Thanks for coming! Please come again!"

Jack nodded awkwardly, as he wasn't sure how to respond, but he felt like he had to acknowledge her so he wouldn't be rude. All the way home, Jack berated himself for being so awkward around a girl, but at least she had been nicer than the first one. However, he tried not to think about that. He would rather focus on how embarrassing he had acted towards Heather. Still he resolved to return to Heather's store the next time he needed something, whether he had his license back or not.

He also wondered about Heather's sister, Barbara. Heather had mentioned that she was a bat, but he wondered how much was she like a bat? Did she have wings? Could she fly? His head was overflowing with questions, which was a nice distraction as he walked home, but he decided that he wouldn't pester Heather for answers. After all she hadn't pestered him with questions about being a wolf.

For now he would just have to be content with the fact that he wasn't the only Anthro in Rawling, even though it seemed like it so far. And he wasn't the only one Buchannon was making his offer to, which only made him more suspicious in Jack's eyes. As he climbed the stairs to his apartment, Jack wondered if Barbara had accepted the offer or not.

Heather hadn't really said whether she had, only that she hadn't gotten the weird feeling about it. Jack sighed as he entered his apartment and decided that maybe it was best if he didn't know the answer. He tossed the shopping bags on the table and headed for his bed. All he could think about right now was a nap; he had had enough excitement for one day.

Chapter 6: Back to Work

The next few days passed slowly, just as Jack had thought they would, but finally Friday, the day of his check-up and license test, arrived. Jack had been practicing driving with his dad every day since he got out of the hospital. In fact it was the only thing that kept him from going stir crazy in his little apartment and it helped keep his mind off his condition. He looked forward to his dad's visits every day after he got off work. They would spend several hours driving around so Jack could get used to driving with his new body.

Everything came to him fairly easy, as he had been an excellent driver before becoming an Anthro. Although there was one thing that took some getting used to: his legs. His feet were considerably larger than before, and his multi-jointed legs were awkward to move in the tight confines of the driver's seat of his truck. Both made it more difficult to drive than before. It took a lot of practice before Jack became comfortable driving with his new body.

By Friday Jack was driving his truck almost as easily as he had before, and he felt confident that he would pass his test. Jack hoped nothing would happen at the DMV because he dreaded getting yelled at again, like at the convenience store. He wasn't sure what would happen if he couldn't get his license back. Also, he didn't want to think about what his dad might do if someone at the DMV were to treat him like the woman in the store had.

Jack's dad arrived with plenty of time for them to get to the hospital before his appointment. He even let Jack drive, so he could get in some last-minute practice before his test later that day. At the hospital, they took him back to an exam room almost immediately, and Jack found himself waiting what felt like hours for Dr. Hawthorn.

In reality Jack only sat in the room for about five minutes by himself before the doctor arrived. Dr. Hawthorn asked him a few questions, like do you have any residual pain or numbness? Any trouble walking or reaching? How are you adapting to your new body?

Jack expected all the doctor's questions and had thought out his answers ready, so they got through all the questions quickly. Next the doctor gave him a physical and checked all his reflexes and joints to make sure that everything was as it should be. Before he knew it, Jack was being led out to the waiting area to get his papers, so he could go back to work on Monday.

He had been worried about his check-up, but the doctor told him as he left that he had done very well and that he wouldn't need to come back for a second check-up. This was unusual as most Anthros did, Dr. Hawthorn explained. His dad was surprised to see him so quickly, but he jumped up, and they both headed out the door. Jack was questioned for a second time on the way to the DMV, as his dad asked him about what Hawthorn had said. After answering all his dad's questions, Jack and his dad sat in silence, which was rare with his dad, who normally loved to talk while driving.

Although he probably knew that Jack was nervous about his test, so it wasn't that out of character for him, given the situation. His dad couldn't have known the extent of Jack's nervousness though, as he hadn't told him or his mom about the incident at the store. Jack's biggest fear at that moment was that someone, or worse, more than one person at the DMV, would act in a similar manner as the store cashier. He was also still worried about what his dad might do, or say, if someone were even half as vocal as that woman had been.

He took a deep breath as his dad parked at the DMV, and his dad gave him a reassuring pat on the back. They walked in, and Jack immediately felt all the eyes in the room turn and stare at him. The large room that took up most of the building was lined with chairs, and along the far wall was a long counter where the employees sat. Thankfully Jack noticed that he wasn't the only Anthro in the place as seated towards the back row of chairs there were not one but two Anthros.

The first appeared to be male, based on the clothes he wore, and looked like a large brown bear, and the other was female and resembled a small corgi dog. She smiled at Jack and his dad, who took this small gesture as an invitation to sit by her. Jack's dad immediately struck up a conversation with the corgi Anthro as well, but Jack's attention was drawn to the Anthro bear sitting at the other end of the row.

He was sitting with his arms crossed and was staring angrily at the screen that displayed the ticket numbers as they were called. Currently the number read fifty-seven, then suddenly jumped to fifty-eight. The bear Anthro got up, angrily huffing, and after approaching the counter, complained loudly to the man behind the counter about having to wait for so long. Of course the employee behind the counter did his best to calm him down. But the bear Anthro continued to complain as he and another employee with a clip board headed to the parking lot for his test.

Jack assumed that the corgi Anthro was also here for the test just as he was, and his dad confirmed this as Jack turned his attention back to them. He glanced at his own ticket and saw that the number read sixty-six, which meant that they were going to be waiting for a while.

It was at this moment that the corgi Anthro turned to Jack and asked, "So...I'm sorry for being so blunt but...I was just wondering what kind of dog you were? I mean you don't look like any breed I've ever seen."

"Oh...well..." Jack wasn't sure how to answer her because he was still upset by his status as an Anthro, and she had caught him off guard. He decided it was best to just correct her assumption and leave it at that, "I'm not actually a dog. I'm a wolf."

"Oh..." She seemed genuinely surprised. "...I'm sorry. I didn't mean to assume, but your personality didn't strike me as a wolf."

He waved her apology away. Her answer sounded genuine, and Jack didn't detect any sarcasm in her words, but it still struck Jack as slightly offensive for some reason. Was there really a personality you could attach to an animal? None of the ones for a wolf seemed to be good, as far as Jack thought. Did she think that, for him to be a wolf Anthro, he had to be aggressive, loud, or rude, and since he wasn't, he had to be a dog?

Jack didn't think there was anything wrong with being a dog Anthro, simply being an Anthro was bad enough. For some reason though, his pride was hurt by her words. As if it were a bad thing that she had assumed he was a dog. He tried to push the thought out of his head and ignore it; after all it was just a simple misunderstanding.

Still the entire exchange left Jack feeling awkward and uncomfortable, and he sat in silence as his dad and the corgi Anthro continued their conversation. Sometime later it felt like an eternity to Jack. The girl's number, sixty-three, flashed onto the screen, and she jumped up from her seat.

"Wish me luck!" she giggled as she walked to the counter. Jack's dad nudged him as she walked away, and he winked at Jack.

"What?" Jack asked, slightly confused.

"Don't what me, boy..." his dad shot back with a grin. "I was trying to get you a date! But you just sat there!"

"What? With her?" Jack asked dismissively, not wanting to give his dad any more reason to embarrass him.

He knew that if he showed even the slightest hint of interest, his dad would ask her on a date for him. This would, of course, be both awkward and embarrassing for Jack, and it wouldn't be the first time his dad had done it either. Jack had learned that the best way to avoid this outcome would be to pretend that he wasn't interested in the girl at all. However, his dad had gotten very good at telling if Jack liked a girl or not, so it wasn't easy.

In this particular instance, however, Jack had the upper hand, as his dad wouldn't be able to read his emotions as easily thanks to him now being an Anthro. But it was also the fact that both he and the girl were Anthros that made Jack want nothing to do with her. How could he love a dog? And how could he be with someone who loved him, even though he was a wolf?

It just wasn't right, and no matter how much he tried, he didn't think he would ever be attracted to any Anthro. Just one more thing the Virus had taken from him, he thought. He had no chance of finding a girlfriend looking like he did now.

Jack was interested in girls and dating, but he didn't want his dad asking someone out on a date for him. As if he didn't have a hard-enough time finding dates as it was. He didn't need people assuming he was a loser or weird because his dad was asking girls out on his behalf.

He just had a hard time working up the courage to ask girls out, and he probably missed a lot of opportunities in the past because of it. Not to mention how awkward he usually was, even when he wasn't trying to get a date. Ultimately Jack knew his dad was just trying to help, so he couldn't get too upset with him.

Luckily Jack wouldn't be around when the girl came back as his number flashed on the screen. He got up, and his dad gave him an over enthusiastic thumbs up. Jack smiled and rolled his eyes; his dad was always good at breaking the tension. The instructor who would give him his test stood behind the counter as he approached. Seeing Jack his eyes grew wide for a second before returning to normal, and Jack felt a pit open in his stomach.

Jack greeted the instructor, who half-heartedly returned it. Then Jack handed him his paperwork and license. The instructor looked over everything quickly and nodded his head.

"Good, you've got everything in order, that should make things go quicker," he said, sounding only half interested in what he was doing and his earlier shock seeming to have completely disappeared.

He worried that the instructor's attitude meant that he was going to fail him no matter what. Jack persevered and completed the test as best he could and felt that he had done a good job on it. Thankfully Jack's fears were unfounded, and the instructor, despite his off-putting attitude, passed him.

Now with the okay from his doctor and his license back, he could finally return to work. He was also happy to see as he walked back into the DMV that the corgi Anthro was gone. Although he hoped it was because, like him, she had passed her test and not because she had failed it.

Even though he was eager to return to work and some sense of normality, Jack couldn't help but be overcome with a sense of dread and loathing. After all no one else had seen him since he went to the hospital, and he feared they might treat him the same as the cashier had. Despite this fear, he still felt as if a weight had been lifted from his shoulders. And he could breathe a little easier knowing that he had a clean bill of health and could drive again.

The weekend passed quickly, as it always seems to, and Jack would soon find out if his fears and worries were warranted or not. Monday morning he got up early. After a brief stop at the convenience store for an energy drink and a quick chat with Heather for encouragement, he headed to work. An all-to-familiar knot forming in his stomach. Parking in his usual spot, Jack took a few minutes to collect himself and mentally prepare for what was to come.

Jack took a deep breath and got out of his truck, grabbing his lunch as he went. Heading into the building, he glanced nervously around. Seeing that the other guys on the maintenance crew were already there, as their respective vehicles were already parked in their usual spaces.

He wasn't sure if that was good or bad, but he tried not to think about it too much. As he opened the door to the building, he heard voices talking loudly and recognized them as his coworkers. The second he opened the door, the loud squeak of the old door announced his entrance, and the group suddenly went quiet.

Thanks to the open floor plan of the building, Jack had walked into the main bay at the back of which his coworkers stood idly chatting as they waited to clock in. The three men stood around the break table where they would return to eat lunch and to clock out at the end of the day. However, all three had noticed him enter and now stared in his direction. Jack had hoped for a more subtly way to ease them into seeing him for the first time, remembering how Mary had first reacted. Unfortunately any plan he may have had was now pointless as the three now stood staring at him from across the bay.

He approached the break table slowly with his head down, hoping to avoid their stares for as long as possible. Jack sheepishly managed a greeting, raising his hand and head slightly, unintentionally meeting the gaze of the man closest to him, CJ. CJ was an older man with a bald head and prominent salt and pepper beard.

To Jack's surprise, CJ smiled and clapped him on the back, saying, "Welcome back, bud! Good to see you! Still can't believe you and Mary stuck it out for as long as you did...the schools being closed and all..." he trailed off, glancing over at the other two, who were still staring at Jack.

Chuck was the oldest of the three, and he glared at Jack. His wrinkled face was weathered and his long, white hair was pulled back into a loose ponytail. Jack also noticed he was the only one of them not wearing a mask, other than himself. There was a moment of awkward silence before he finally spoke, his voice abrasive and rough.

"What?! Are we just supposed to ignore the fact that he's an animal?! Just going to sweep that under the rug, huh?! Just pretend everything's back to normal?! Never mind that we could all be dead tomorrow and it'd be because those morons that run this place let that thing in here with us?! I knew I should've listened to Dean and quit like he did! Lot of good it did him..."

Chuck's words cut Jack like a knife. He couldn't decide if he wanted to throw up, run away, or punch Chuck. Or at the very least he couldn't decide which to do first or in what order. Luckily CJ spoke up as Chuck opened his mouth to continue his tirade.

"Now Chuck, I don't think that kind of talk is called for! Jack's a good kid, and given what he's been thorough, he deserves some sympathy. Besides, it's not his fault he got sick, in fact if it's anyone's fault, it's ours for not being here when we could have. If we had, maybe Jack wouldn't have gotten sick! And Dean getting sick was terrible, but just because he didn't make it and Jack did doesn't mean you can blame Jack!"

Jack was surprised by CJ's use of the word "sick." After all he hadn't heard anyone refer to him as such since leaving the hospital. Even if it was true, Jack had been allowed to come home only because he was no longer infectious, whether Chuck believed it or not. The news about their coworker's fate also struck Jack hard. It still a strange feeling to survive something so deadly, and he definitely felt a little guilty about it.

Chuck waved a hand dismissively at CJ and walked into the adjoining bay where the mowers were kept. CJ returned it with one of his own and made a face at the older man behind his back as he disappeared through the door. As they watched him leave, the third man, who was a new employee that Jack didn't recognize, stepped closer to Jack. He looked young, with medium-length blond hair and a large, crooked nose that appeared to have been broken at some time in his past. The man stared in awe at him, then started to speak, his voice low and cool.

"Wow! How cool is that! So you're like a wolf or something, huh? That's cool." He was clearly excited to be talking to an Anthro. "Does your fur make it hard to wear clothes? Can you howl like a wolf? Do you only eat meat? Can you eat normal food?" He went on asking, but Jack found his quick-fire questions far too overwhelming. "My name's Brett, by the way..." he trailed off, asking more questions.

CJ opened his mouth to tell Brett to stop, but he didn't have to as the door opened again, and Mary walked in with an unexpected shadow. The superintendent of King County School District, Dr. Earl Rose, was following close behind her. He seemed oddly out of place in the garage with his neat grey suit and black tie. His dark hair neatly combed to hide an obvious bald spot and a pair of glasses perched on his nose.

"Hello, everyone!" Mary called, walking towards them followed by the superintendent.

No one said anything as she approached, wary of why Dr. Rose was there. She looked at them with what Jack thought was a reassuring look, as if to say, "No one's in trouble," but it was hard to tell since she was wearing a mask. Which only made Rose's visit more unusual.

"Dr. Rose wanted to welcome Jack back personally," Mary explained, and it looked like she was about to say more but was cut off by Rose, whose voice was nasally and slightly high pitched.

"Yes indeed! On behalf of the entire district, I wanted to welcome you back after your long absence! I also wanted to reassure you that you will be treated no differently than you were before! If you were to be discriminated against by any employee, I would hope that you would report it immediately to the proper individuals within the district."

He adjusted his own mask as he finished his speech with a slight smile. Jack knew the speech was more for legal reasons than any real compassion on the superintendent's part. Rose was, no doubt, more worried about being sued than anything else. Still Jack thanked him and politely excused himself from the conversation.

Jack had no intention of reporting anything, as he greatly disliked conflict and preferred not to make waves if he could help it. His only real goal was to keep his head down and do his job until things settled back down to something closer to normal. This would prove difficult as Chuck had already shown his displeasure at having to work with him, and he doubted his attitude would improve over time.

Over the next few weeks, Jack settled into the routine of avoiding Chuck and Brett as much as he could. He didn't want to hurt Brett's feelings, but his questions seemed never-ending and were becoming more personal, and as far as Jack was concerned, inappropriate. Chuck, on the other hand, had taken to trying to get him in trouble or fired as often as possible. As well as just being rude to him whenever he got the chance.

CJ and Mary were the only ones who seemed to treat him the same as they had before. Even the teachers and other staff at the schools seemed to be either avoiding him or disgusted by his presence and made it very clear how they felt. It was the little things that Jack noticed more than anything.

Teachers who had waved to him or greeted him in the mornings as he mowed now looked the other way or pretend they didn't see him when they clearly did. The other staff he would normally see during the day, like the custodians who started work as he was leaving for the evening, would tolerate him talking to them. But would often be agitated or short with him as they entered their respective buildings.

It was because of this treatment from his coworkers that Jack would begin to avoid them altogether. Mary and CJ tried their best to help Jack whenever they could, but they were fighting a losing battle. Jack supposed he couldn't blame everyone, after all many of them were still worried about the Virus, and Jack, being an Anthro, was an easy target for their hatred, disgust, and fear.

Jack was beginning to reconsider Buchannon's offer after weeks of being treated so poorly, despite how he felt about Anthros. He appreciated Mary and CJ's attempts to cheer him up or make things easier for him, but he still spent most of his workday in a depressed slump. Of course he still felt uneasy about the Claw Creek offer, but he knew he couldn't take much more from people who were supposed to be his friends and coworkers.

Chapter 7: Quarantine

After parking his truck in his usual spot one morning, Jack sat there listening to the quiet. He loved the silence of the early morning and had made a habit of sitting in his truck for a few minutes every morning to prepare himself for the day ahead of him. After taking a few deep breaths, he grabbed his lunch box and headed inside.

The morning passed quickly, and Jack felt like he was in a haze, just coasting along on autopilot till lunch. As he sat down at the break table, he was joined by both CJ and Mary. They had started sitting with him at lunch in a small attempt at make him feel less alone, but it didn't really help.

They sat quietly eating their lunches and listening to the radio. Jack felt awkward sitting with them. Mostly because they were all sitting quietly and not talking, which was also unusual as both greatly enjoyed chatting while they took their breaks.

Today, though, they both sat in silence, the radio quietly playing in the background. Suddenly the trio heard the radio let out the all too familiar warning tone that proceeded emergency broadcasts. Jack felt uneasy as the voice belted out its message.

"Attention! This is a message from the CDC concerning the Roderick Virus. New research into the Virus and its properties has revealed a possible strain, or strains, that continue to be contagious after advancing to Stage Two. All individuals who have entered Stage Two and have been released from the hospital are to report immediately to the nearest hospital for quarantine."

The message repeated before the warning tone returned and the radio went back to normal as Jack, Mary, and CJ sat in silence. Could it be possible that Jack had been unintentionally infecting everyone at the school? He wasn't sure but knew that he wasn't about to risk infecting anyone else. Jumping up from his seat, Jack rushed towards the door, apologizing profusely to both of his coworkers as they, too, jumped up from their seats. CJ and Mary assured him that he had nothing to apologize for, and they both wished him luck at the hospital as he hurried off.

Jack's heart was in his throat as he drove to the hospital. He didn't want to even consider the possibility that he was still contagious. Unfortunately that was all he could think about as he sped towards the hospital. Pulling into the parking lot of the hospital sometime later, he took a minute to calm himself down before he went inside. After a few deep breaths, he felt his pulse slow somewhat and got out of his truck.

He ran a hand over the top of his head as he walked into the hospital. A nervous tick he had from when he had hair instead of fur. Walking quickly up to the receptionist, he opened his mouth to explain why he was there. She cut him off by pointing to a box of surgical masks on the counter in front of her. Jack quickly put one on as the receptionist called for a nurse.

The mask was somewhat ill fitting for his snout, but he thought it was better than nothing. A nurse came out from behind a set of doors and led him back to one of the exam rooms, not unlike one of the ones he was put in when he first came to the hospital. Jack also recognized the nurse as one of the many who tended to him while he was going through his change. He sat on the paper lined bed, and the nurse took his temperature.

"Do you know about the quarantine?" she asked as she placed a blood pressure cuff on his arm.

"Yes, that's why I'm here," he answered, feeling the cuff tighten around his arm.

"Good. I'm glad you had the sense to come in. You wouldn't believe how many Anthros have already called in to say that they were just going to stay at home," she said, sounding flustered and annoyed as she released the pressure on the cuff and took it off his arm.

"Well I can understand why they wouldn't want to...after what they went through here..." Jack said, trying to sympathize with them.

The nurse looked at him for a second, then said, "Well I guess I can see that, but I would think that they would rather sit in a hospital than possibly infect anyone and everyone they might come in contact with."

"True," Jack agreed. "After all that's exactly why I came in as soon as I heard the broadcast."

"I hope they come to their senses soon and come in," she said. "I'd hate it if their families, or the police if it came to that, had to go door to door to get Anthros to come in here..." She trailed off and gave a slight shudder at the thought.

"I hope it doesn't come to that, too," Jack agreed.

"Well, on that note, the doctor will be in shortly to talk to you about the quarantine and the steps we need to take to ensure more people don't get sick," she said as she turned to leave, giving him a smile as she left the room.

In spite of the situation, Jack couldn't help but think of what his dad would say if he had been there. Probably something about how he should have asked the nurse out or something. Jack sat in the room for some time before Dr. Hawthorn came in, no doubt busy with patients and Anthros coming in because of the quarantine. When he did, he looked exhausted but gave Jack a big smile as he sat down in front of the computer the nurse had been entering his vitals in.

"Mr. Towzer! How are you? Been adjusting to things?" he asked politely.

"Fine," Jack answered, not really wanting to bother with small talk.

"Well, if it's any consolation, I'm glad to see you can follow instructions," he said, his smile disappearing for a moment, and Jack nodded in agreement.

"First I suppose we should discuss the findings that led to the quarantine..." Dr. Hawthorn began, "...A series of tests that were conducted by scientists studying the Roderick Virus seemed to show that at least one mutated strain of the Virus could possibly continue being contagious. Infecting others after the individual had entered, or even after they had endured, Stage Two. More tests will still be needed to confirm anything, but the CDC and hospitals around the world are taking no chances and called for a full quarantine of any and all individuals at or beyond Stage Two." Dr. Hawthorn looked at Jack for a moment before asking, "Any questions so far?" To which Jack shook his head, and the doctor continued his explanation, "Now the tests will take a long time to run, and it could be weeks or even months before they've determined anything. Government officials are currently working to set up quarantine zones at various places across the country, but it will take time to get it all together. A more...long-term solution exists, but I doubt many Anthros would agree to it who hadn't already."

"What's their long-term solution?" Jack asked, fairly certain he knew where Hawthorn was going but allowed the doctor to explain.

"The long-term solution is to send Anthros to one of the Anthro communities that have been popping up all over the country. For example the nearest one to us is called Claw Creek..." Hawthorn was cut off by someone knocking sharply on the door. They had both jumped at the same time. Jack jumped at the mention of Claw Creek, but Dr. Hawthorn jumped at the sudden knock on the door, and he quickly got up to answer it. "Perfect timing, Councilor Morgan!" he said as he opened the door.

A tall Anthro with the features of a lioness walked in. She held herself with a quiet dignity and grace that made it plainly obvious that she was someone of great importance. But strangely she lacked the over-the-top nature of Buchannon. Dr. Hawthorn excused himself from the room as she sat down.

"Hello, Mr.... Towzer, correct?" she asked, holding her hand out to Jack.

"Yes, ma'am. Jack Towzer," Jack answered, feeling slightly intimidated as he shook her hand.

"My name is Lucy Morgan, and I am the current elected official in charge of the Anthro community known as Claw Creek," she explained. "I understand you spoke to one of my representatives before your release from this hospital several weeks ago?"

"Yes, ma'am. I spoke to Jason Buchannon," Jack answered but immediately wished he hadn't as the Councilor's expression changed to one of pure disgust.

"Buchannon...yes, that was what I thought," she said, clearly still unhappy. "You should know that Mr. Buchannon has been removed from his position. I won't go into too much detail now, but suffice it to say that he was caught embezzling from the town and will be persecuted to the fullest extent of the law."

"Oh, I see..." Jack said awkwardly, not sure how to respond.

"But that's not what I came here to discuss with you," Morgan continued, sounding less angry. "I wanted to talk to you about becoming a resident of our community. Now I know you never gave a definitive answer when you talked to Buchannon, but I would like to make you a more...formal...offer than whatever Buchannon had promised."

Jack was somewhat relieved to hear about Buchannon. At least knowing that he hadn't just been getting a weird feeling from him because he was an Anthro made him feel a little better about not accepting the deal he had been offered. He figured that Buchannon was probably taking money from the new residents as a fake tax or something like that. Besides, now he knew that the Anthros running the town were at least trying to do a good job and look out for its residents.

"I understand from Buchannon's notes on your conversation that you had talked about being a farmer?" Morgan went on. "Well we certainly need more if we want to be a more self-sufficient community. Currently we only have one, a dairy farmer named Fred Nelson and his family. What were you thinking of doing, growing crops, raising animals, or both?"

Jack began explaining what he had always imagined his life on a farm would entail. He explained how he had always wanted to raise beef cattle and how he had planned to grow corn and other grains to feed the cattle. As well as how he also wanted to raise pigs and possibly even chickens but on a much smaller scale than the cattle.

After he had finished his explanation, Morgan smiled and said, "Well you certainly seem to have put a lot of thought into this, that's good. But I don't want you to rush into anything, so think it over and talk to your parents or anyone else you might need or want to."

"Right," Jack said, "I was already planning to."

"Good." She continued, "We can work out all the details later, for now I have a property in mind for you that I want to look into more closely before we get into more specifics. If you'll come to Claw Creek, I'm sure we can find a place for you. I just wish we could have met under more... relaxed circumstances. And I don't want you to feel like you must take the farm offer just to get out of going to one of the quarantine sites because you don't. We have plenty of apartments for rent if you'd rather just live there till the quarantine is lifted. I don't want to take up too much of your time, so I'll leave things up to you for now."

"Well thank you very much for the offer. It was a pleasure to talk to you, and I will definitely talk things over with my parents and let you know either way," Jack said, feeling that he had finally gotten some good news.

They both stood and shook hands again. The Councilor handed him a business card with her number on it. Then told him to call her personally if he had any questions or concerns.

Jack waited until the sound of her footsteps disappeared down the hall before calling his parents and telling them about everything that had happened. He talked to them for a time but had to cut their conversation short as Dr. Hawthorn returned to check in on him. After making sure everything was okay, Hawthorn had Jack moved to an overnight room in what had become the quarantine wing of the hospital. Which was meant to hold Anthros before they were moved to either a community or one of the quarantine sites. It was only after they had signed several wavers and been suited up in hazmat suits again that his parents could visit him in his room.

They continued their conversation and ultimately came to a collective decision. Jack would accept the offer to move to Claw Creek and look at the supposed property. If it was to Jack's liking, he could accept the offer or not, his parents left it completely up to him.

However, all three agreed that, at worst, he would accept the offer to live in an apartment in Claw Creek until the quarantine was lifted. Then if he wanted, move back to Rawling after it was over. Either way he would be forced to quit his job at the school. If the quarantine took months to lift, and Jack couldn't go back to work until it was, it seemed almost inevitable that he would be fired anyway.

Jack's dad, however, liked the idea of Jack being able to use the quarantine to his advantage and fulfill his dream of being a farmer. In other words, turning a negative situation into a positive one. Of course he would still have to be cautious, so he wouldn't be cheated or tricked in any way. Even though it seemed like the troublemaker Buchannon had been stopped already, he was still cautious.

The following day, Jack called the Councilor and told her his decision. She was very happy to hear it and promised that she would personally escort him to Claw Creek. Councilor Morgan arrived roughly an hour later, and after he and his parents signed several documents so Jack could be released from the hospital, they were off. Jack and Morgan climbed into a van that was labeled "QUARANTINE" and had large quarantine symbols all over it while his parents went home, as they were not allowed in any designated quarantine zone like Claw Creek.

Chapter 8: Claw Creek

As they rode in the van, Morgan told Jack all about Claw Creek, some of which he had already heard from Buchannon, but there was plenty that he had left out of his little speech. She told him about how, before the quarantine, many Anthros and their families had moved to Claw Creek and were happy there. Unfortunately, after the quarantine, many of the Anthro's human families had to move away, as it had been declared a quarantine site and no non-Anthros were allowed within a mile of the small town.

She also told him about the Nelson family, who she had mentioned earlier. The patriarch of the family, Fred Nelson, was one of the founders of Claw Creek and even donated a sizable portion of the land for the town from his own property. He was also considered to be a kind and helpful man by nearly all the residents of the town. His family was also somewhat unique as the entire family had become Anthros, something that was almost unheard of. They were also all cattle Anthros, a somewhat ironic twist as they were dairy farmers.

Other notable residents of the town included the McGregor family, who had just recently opened a farm store. The family consisted of just two people, Flint McGregor, an older goat Anthro who walked with a cane, and Chad McGregor, his son who was a horse Anthro and quite the troublemaker around town apparently. Besides them other notable people included the owner of one of the local bars, Evelyn Kitt, a hyena Anthro who had opened a bar with her human parents but now ran it alone since the quarantine forced them to leave, Nikki Whitefield, the local police officer who was a Doberman Anthro, and the Rowe family, who owned the local grocery store. Rebecca Rowe, the daughter and a tiger shark Anthro, was the one most of the townspeople saw as she was the cashier.

Jack tried to make mental notes of all the prominent people of the town but knew he would probably forget most of what Morgan told him. Still it was nice to have an idea of what the people in town were like. He was more worried about the property they were going to look at though and that he would have to decide on his own whether to buy the property or not since his parents couldn't be there with him.

Before too long they arrived at the town, passing through a quarantine check point before entering. It was a small town, but it was well-built. Most of the buildings were new of course, but they weren't crammed together or spread far apart. They drove slowly through the town, and Jack was able to pick out a few landmarks, like the grocery and farm stores.

They turned west and headed through the town, and Morgan pointed out the Claw Creek Dairy Farm, the Nelson family's farm, which took up the western border of the town, then they turned around and headed back into the town. After coming to the center of town, they turned south and headed for the edge of town again. This time stopping in front of an old farmhouse which stood in the middle of a field.

It was clearly vacant with the grass growing up quite high in the yard and the various fields standing empty. All the dilapidated fences needed repairs and the old barn, which stood a little way from the house, needed repairs as well. Jack noted that several metal sheets on the barn roof were loose and lifted slightly every time the wind blew.

The van pulled into the driveway and parked near the house. Jack and Morgan got out, and Morgan led Jack up to the house. Up the small front steps, onto the equally small porch, to the front door.

"This is it," Morgan said as she turned the key in the lock and opened the front door. "I know it isn't much now, but with a little cleaning and repairs, I think this place will be a great fit for you."

Jack nodded, looking around and surveying everything from ceiling to floor. The entryway was set up as a mud room with a tiled floor and space for boots on the floor, hooks for coats, and a small wall shelf for gloves or other small items that would be kept there. Leading from there was a stairway to the second floor, which consisted of a hallway that led to all three small bedrooms. Next to the stairs was a hallway that led to the kitchen, which consisted of a set of old-looking appliances and a well-used stainless-steel sink. In the hallway to the kitchen, there was a doorway leading to the living room and a door leading to the bathroom.

The bathroom had a shower, sink, and toilet that looked like they had been there since before the house was even built, but Morgan assured him that all functioned perfectly. As for the living room, it was spacious with a large picture window taking up most of the wall at the front of the house. It was also completely empty, containing no furniture or any indication that it had ever had anything in it at all.

Morgan took out a file and began reading the list of repairs the house needed. It was quite a bit but nothing Jack thought he couldn't handle. Things like loose floorboards and a few rooms needing to be painted. The biggest challenge lay outside.

The fences around the various fields would need many boards replaced, and in some places, entire sections of fence needed to be torn out and replaced. Of course all the fences and barn would need to be painted, too. As far as the barn was concerned, the loose sheets of metal on the roof and some of the boards in the hay loft would have to be replaced. In all Jack felt like all the repairs would be manageable, they would just take time. The house was livable as it was, and the barn and fences could be done little by little.

Morgan showed Jack throughout the house and out to the barn, and they even walked around some of the nearby fences. Jack was surprised that the Councilor was comfortable walking around the farm, but it seemed to not bother her at all. She even seemed to enjoy it, and Jack wondered if she had grown up on a farm or had worked on one when she was younger. He thought it was best not to ask though, as he didn't want to say something insensitive or awkward.

As they walked back to the van, they saw a large dark red pickup truck pull in and park near it. The door of the truck swung open, and a large bull Anthro stepped out. He had short, slightly curved horns atop his head, short dark brown fur, and wore a slightly dirty-looking pair of blue jeans and a red plaid button up shirt. Fred Nelson waved and smiled at Jack and Morgan as they approached him.

"Well hello there!" he called, his voice booming but cheerful. "I was hoping I would catch you two out here." Fred shook both of their hands eagerly and asked, "So you're Jack Towzer? Thought you'd be taller..." he laughed at his own joke and clapped Jack on the back.

Morgan and Jack both laughed as well, and Jack immediately understood why Fred was so well liked in Claw Creek. Being so large, he was slightly intimidating, but his lighthearted and happy demeanor showed he was both approachable and kind. Fred and Morgan talked for some time before Fred got back to why he had come out to the farm in the first place,

"Anyway," he continued, "I just wanted to stop out and say hello. See what you thought of the old place."

"I like it," Jack answered. "It needs some work, but all in all, I think it'll be perfect for me."

As he said this, both Fred and Morgan smiled. He had been thinking about it since he and Morgan had arrived, and the more of the farm he saw, the more he liked it. Jack was never one to shy away from a little hard work, and he didn't think he would get another chance to buy a farm. At least not one of this size or one for the steeply discounted price they were offering. It wouldn't be easy of course, as there was still a lot of paperwork, loan applications, and the financing would have to be sorted out before anything was official.

"That's great news, Jack!" Morgan said, clearly very happy. "If you'd like, we can go straight to the bank and get all the paperwork and financing started today?"

"That sounds great," Jack replied, wanting to get started as soon as possible. He knew that these kinds of things could take a while to work out all the little details.

"Well don't let me hold you up," Fred said cheerfully. "Oh, and if you need any help with anything around here," he waved his hand vaguely around the place, "you just let me know, okay?" He took out a small scrap of paper and quickly wrote his phone number on it, then handed it to Jack, saying, "I mean it, Jack. Don't you hesitate to give me a call if you need help or have any questions, alright?"

"Okay, I will, thank you," Jack assured him, slipping the paper in his pocket.

"Good, I'll stop by again in a few days to see how you're getting along," Fred said, smiling, and then he got in his truck and drove off.

After Fred had left, Jack and Morgan headed for the bank. They spent the rest of the day there, and after hours of going over all the legal, financing, and loan paperwork, Jack felt both mentally and physically drained. Finally the banker, a squat opossum Anthro, told them that everything seemed to be in order and they would call when everything was filed.

Morgan took Jack back to the farm. She showed him that while they had been away, movers had delivered his things from his apartment in Rawling, including his truck. Then she told him she would stop by again when the paperwork was filed and the farm was officially his.

She also encouraged him to spend the next few days unpacking and settling in. Jack watched her leave and returned her wave as she left. He thought to himself as he watched her leave. It was strange that the entire time he had been in Claw Creek, he hadn't been nearly as upset or bothered by the fact that he was literally surrounded by other Anthros, by animals. Maybe it was just the fact that he was able to distract himself with the farm and unpacking.

Or maybe because he wasn't surrounded by normal people to remind him of his status as an Anthro. The strange feeling that had been plaguing him, however, was still present and as strong as ever, which slightly worried Jack. Either way he quickly settled into his new home. He set up his bed, and after making it, laid down on top of the covers and quickly fell asleep.

Jack woke up early the next morning, and after going through the various boxes, began unpacking what he could. He didn't see the point in unpacking boxes that would go in rooms that needed larger repairs or painting, as they would only get in the way and need to be moved. So he unpacked what he could, starting with the larger furniture that had been brought in and piled up in the living room. Thankfully the living room needed little more than a coat of paint, so Jack just set everything up a few feet away from the walls. The small couch, coffee table, and TV were really all that went in the room anyway, so there was plenty of room.

In fact Jack realized that because the farmhouse was much bigger than his apartment, the room looked extremely bare. Even with all his furniture in place and kept away from the walls. He could always get more things to make the room seem less bare, but he decided to worry about that later.

Next he tackled the kitchen, which like the living room, was much larger than the one in his apartment. His table, which he had always considered large for his apartment, seemed like little more than a small end table in the large kitchen. Jack spent a lot more time than he thought he would just putting away all the food that his parents had filled his apartment with when he came back from the hospital and that he hadn't eaten much of since then.

When he was finished, he took a minute to look around the house and take it all in. It hadn't really hit him the day before just what he was doing, but now the magnitude of it hit him like a freight train. After years of planning, saving, and dreaming, he was finally doing it; he was finally going to live his dream of being a farmer.

He hadn't thought it was possible, and it wasn't how he had been planning it, but it was happening. Jack looked out the window of his bedroom, which overlooked the front of the property and sighed. There was a lot of work to be done, and he didn't intend to start being lazy now.

Jack decided the quickest things he could fix would be the many areas where the walls were chipped or cracked and the several rooms needing a fresh coat of paint. He also decided to buy some nails for the loose floorboards. Even if he didn't take the time to fix them all now, at least he would have them when he needed them later. This would allow him to unpack most of the remaining boxes and be a good way to jump start his restoration of the farmhouse.

To do this, however, Jack needed plaster for the damaged walls, paint, paint brushes, paint rollers, and various other small tools to help him complete the project. He of course had none of these things and would have to go out and get them. Which would mean Jack would have to make his first trip into town, specifically to McGregor's farm store.

Chapter 9: McGregor

Jack grabbed his keys off the hook by the door where the movers had left them and headed out the door. He took a minute to collect his thoughts and take another look at the old farmhouse. It still seemed like a dream, but it wasn't; if it were, he wouldn't have had to endure all that he had to get there. Shaking the negative thoughts from his head, Jack climbed into his truck and headed for McGregor's store.

McGregor's Farm and Hardware was at the center of Claw Creek, along with the Claw Creek Bank, police station, and the grocery store, Creekside Markets. As Jack pulled into the parking lot, he remembered what Morgan had told him about the McGregor's. He hoped that the son, Chad, either wasn't there or wouldn't give him any trouble. Unfortunately, as Jack walked inside, he saw the large brown and white horse Anthro standing by the checkout counter talking with a smaller deer Anthro. Both wore dark green vests with the store name in bright yellow.

The deer Anthro was standing behind the counter, looking annoyed, while Chad leaned on it from the opposite side. Chad seemed to be saying something to the deer, but both turned to look at Jack as he entered. He nodded at them and quickly made his way deeper into the store. As he did so, he overheard Chad continue his conversation with the other employee.

"So? When are you gonna introduce me?" he asked smugly.

"I told you no, Chad," the deer answered, clearly annoyed.

"Come on, Al. Just introduce me to her," Chad replied.

"I will never introduce you to my sister, Chad. So just drop it. Stop asking," the deer called Al retorted.

"Fine, whatever," Chad said, clearly agitated. "It's only a matter of time before she hears about me and comes running."

He laughed as he walked away, and Al glared at him as he walked to the back of the store. Jack, who had been looking around for the paint and things he needed, took the opportunity to ask Al where they were since he couldn't seem to find them on his own. As he walked up to the counter, Al turned back from glaring at where Chad had disappeared and gave Jack a smile.

"Hi there, stranger. Name's Alister, but everyone calls me Al," he said as Jack approached.

"Hi, Al, I'm Jack Towzer," Jack returned his greeting.

"You wouldn't happen to be the guy that just bought that old farm outside town yesterday, would you? Fred was just in here not too long-ago telling Mr. McGregor about meeting you yesterday," Al asked.

"Yeah, that's me," Jack answered, only slightly surprised by how fast news had spread of his purchase. "That's actually why I'm here. I need a few things."

"Oh, no problem. I can help you find whatever you need," Al said.

Jack told Al what he needed, and Al led him back towards the back of the store. Luckily Chad seemed to be nowhere around. With Al's help, Jack was able to find everything he needed, and he even got a brief tour of the store. Al showed Jack where everything was, and Jack was surprised by the large selection they had in the small store. As they searched, Al warned Jack about Chad.

"Chad is Mr. McGregor's son and considers himself a ladies' man, and he hits on just about every girl in Claw Creek. He likes to cause trouble and get into fights. He also likes to target Anthros who are new to town, like you, because he thinks most won't have any idea who he is. So it's easier for him to lie, brag, or pick on them."

"Yeah...I've met some guys like that before..." Jack said nodding. "It's best to avoid them if you can...at least in my experience."

"Kind of hard for me to avoid Chad unfortunately..." Al responded.

"Yeah, I guess it's hard when you have to work with him," Jack agreed. "I heard him mention something about your sister?" he asked, trying not to sound interested in Al's sister but more concerned.

"Oh yeah...my little sister is a senior in high school and turned eighteen a few weeks ago. Ever since Chad had found out, well, he hasn't stopped pestering me to introduce him to her. Of course I've been trying very hard to keep Chad from finding out who she is because...well...she isn't a deer Anthro like me, and Chad never bothered to learn my last name. It isn't that I didn't trust her judgement or anything like that, but I don't want her to have to deal with Chad. Especially if he finds out who she is and decides to go looking for her at the school or when she's out with her friends."

"Right, I get it. You're trying to keep her from having to deal with a bad situation. Looking out for her like a brother should," Jack said, even though he didn't have any siblings of his own, he liked to think that he would act the same way in that situation.

Unfortunately, as Al was ringing up his items, Chad reappeared. He still had the hint of a smirk on his long face. As he approached the checkout counter, both Al and Jack noticed him, and both pretended not to see him. It wasn't until Chad walked right up behind Al and put a hand on his shoulder that Al acknowledged his presence,

"What, Chad?" Al asked, clearly still agitated. "Can't you see I'm busy?"

"Oh, don't be so rude, pal," Chad said, grinning. "Why don't you introduce me to the new guy? Since you guys seem so friendly." Al gave a sigh, shot Jack a knowing look, and they both knew Chad was going to try something.

"This is Jack Towzer," Al began. "He just bought the old farm outside town. And before you ask, no, he doesn't have any sisters or girlfriend for you to harass him about."

Jack was glad Al was taking the initiative and trying to stop Chad before he could even get started, but it didn't make much of a difference because Chad replied, "Come on, Al. I'm not some heartless dirt bag that would hit on the new guy's girl or his sister." His grin widened as he said, "No, not me. But I do have to ask, Jack, right? You got a mom, right?" Chad laughed hysterically at his terrible joke.

Jack hoped he was joking at least. As Jack and Al both opened their mouths to retort, they were surprised to see a small, hunched over goat Anthro had appeared behind Chad. He promptly reached up with his cane and smacked Chad on the back of the head.

"Ow! What was that for?!" Chad shouted, clearly more surprised than hurt.

"You know darn well what it was for!" Flint McGregor retorted in a gruff voice. "Is that any way to treat a customer, Charles?"

"No, sir," Chad responded, looking at the floor and rubbing the back of his head.

"Now apologize," Flint insisted.

Chad looked up slightly, then muttered, "Sorry," glancing sideways at both of them, and Jack could see that he was more upset that he had been caught in the act rather than being sorry or remorseful.

"I guess that'll do, boy," Flint said, glaring at Chad. "Now head to the stockroom and finish your jobs back there."

"Yes, sir," Chad replied and hurried to the back of the store again, still rubbing the back of his head.

"Sorry about him, young man," Flint said, turning to face Jack. "He's a handful, but he wasn't always. And hopefully I can knock some sense into him one of these days." Flint laughed as he motioned with his cane.

Al and Jack joined in half-heartedly. Flint McGregor seemed a little odd but meant well. At least Jack thought that that was something Morgan had said to him. Jack introduced himself to the old Anthro, who shook his hand firmly and watched as Al finished ringing up his things.

"Good work, Al, as always," Flint said smiling.

"Thank you, sir," Al said, also smiling.

"As for you, Mr. Towzer, I hope you won't let my son keep you from doing business with us in the future," Flint said, looking at Jack.

"I won't," Jack replied. "Besides, I think between Al and myself, we can handle him just fine." They all smiled, and Flint laughed again.

"I bet you can, and if not, well, my cane certainly can!" he laughed. "Well I had better get back to the stockroom myself. It was nice meeting you, Mr. Towzer, and I hope to see you around the store in the future."

"It was nice meeting you, too, sir," Jack called after him as the old goat made his way slowly to the back of the store.

Jack thanked Al for helping him deal with Chad as he gathered his things. Al brushed it off, saying it was nothing as Jack headed out of the store. He smiled to himself as he drove back to the farm. It felt like some of the weight he had carried with him since the hospital had lifted, and for the first time since then, it felt like things were going to be okay. Maybe he was going to be okay.

Chapter 10: Broken Fences

Jack spent the next few days repairing and painting the walls of the old farmhouse. It was a tedious and tiring job. He started by plastering all the cracks and holes in the walls. Then sanding the plaster smooth once it dried. Finally he taped all the windows, light switches, and electrical outlets so that he wouldn't get paint on them. After doing all that, he was finally ready to paint.

As he had promised, Fred checked in on him several times. Every time he did, he would just start helping Jack with whatever it was that he was doing at that time. It didn't matter if it was plastering, sanding, taping, or painting, Fred would jump right in and start helping him. He also wouldn't accept any sort of payment for his help either. Jack made a mental note to repay Fred in some way when he could.

With Fred's help, Jack was able to get the walls fixed in no time. As he was cleaning up on the last day of painting the final room, which happened to be the living room, his thoughts turned to his next job on the farm. He looked out the window and saw the dilapidated fences outside. The fences and barn both needed major repairs, and Jack had been slightly hesitant to tackle either of them. After finishing his first job though, he felt a new surge of confidence.

Making up his mind to start on the fences, Jack finished cleaning up the painting supplies. He then walked outside to examine the fences and what needed to be replaced or repaired. Starting with the fences closest to the house, he made a checklist of how many boards he would need, as well as what tools he thought he would need.

Satisfied that he had enough information to start on the fences, Jack made his way to his truck. Before he could get there, however, Fred pulled into the driveway. They waved to each other, and Fred stepped out of his truck.

"Jack! I was just stopping by to see if you needed any help today?" Fred explained.

"Actually I was just heading out to get some things to start fixing the fences," Jack answered.

"Well, if you'd like, I could go with you," Fred offered.

Jack had spent enough time with Fred over the last week or so to know that he enjoyed helping Jack and that he wouldn't have offered if he hadn't meant it. Otherwise Jack would have felt bad accepting so much help from him and not giving anything in return.

He smiled at Fred and asked, "Your truck or mine?"

"Well we might as well take mine since it's here," Fred replied smiling.

They both laughed, and Fred motioned for him to get in his truck. Then they rode down to McGregor's, where they were greeted by Al. Al helped them find everything they would need, and the three of them loaded everything into Fred's truck.

As they were getting ready to leave, however, Al asked, "Hey, Jack, if you need another hand, I could stop by this weekend and help out."

Jack was surprised by Al's sudden offer, but it was Fred who answered him, "Of course! The more, the merrier!" he laughed and clapped Al on the back. "Many hands make light work, right?" Fred continued, smiling at Jack, who agreed, "Right. I'll take all the help I can get."

All three of them laughed, and Jack wondered how he could ever repay them. He tried not to think about it too much and focus on the tasks ahead. Jack and Fred returned to the farm with the supplies and unloaded it from the truck. They stacked it all in the dry part of the barn, away from the leaks and holes in the roof.

The two of them spent the rest of the day tearing down any old, rotting fence boards and pulling up any posts that seemed weak or loose. After they had a sizeable portion of the fence prepped, they began planting the new posts and nailing up the new boards. They spent the rest of the week doing the same process over and over. Tearing down the bad sections and putting up the new.

Jack liked working with Fred. He was a hard worker and was always talking and joking with him as they worked. It made the work go quickly, and Jack found himself looking forward to each day, despite the seemingly endless amount of work they had to do. Before he knew it, it was the weekend, and true to his word, Al arrived at the farm early Saturday morning.

"Hey! Hope I'm not late!" Al called as he got out of his car.

"Right on time!" Jack called back, and all three of them laughed.

The three of them surveyed the large section of fence line the two of them had completed during the week. Jack was surprised to see just how much of the fence was done, as he hadn't really been paying attention while he and Fred were working. Still he felt a great sense of accomplishment. Not just because they had gotten so much of the fence done in so little time but also because he felt he had found two good friends in Fred and Al.

Jack found his thoughts wondering to Mary and CJ, after all they were his friends, too. He felt bad as he hadn't really talked to either one since coming to Claw Creek. What were they up to?

How were they coping with the virus? As far as Jack knew, the Virus was still just as widespread as it had been and was showing no signs of slowing down anytime soon. Shaking the thoughts from his head, Jack resolved to give both of them a call after they were done working for the day.

As they worked throughout the morning, Jack discovered that Al was an excellent worker, much like Fred. With Al's help, the three of them were moving quickly through the fence line. In fact they were doing so well, not one of them noticed when it was lunchtime and they had worked straight through. Until midafternoon when Fred happened to notice the time.

"Goodness, look at the time!" he laughed. "We've worked clear through lunch!"

"Huh, guess so," Jack replied, looking at his own watch. "Do you two want to take a break?" he asked, looking to Al and Fred.

"I think that's a good idea," Al answered. "After all we're at a good place to stop."

Which they were, having just finished a long, straight portion of fence that ended at a corner with a gate. Not only were they at a good place to stop, but they had also gotten a lot done. Which was not only because they had an extra set of hands helping them today. It was also a testament to how well the three of them worked together.

"Actually I have a better idea," Jack said. "Since we're at a good place to stop and we did get a lot done today, why don't we quit for the day? We could go out for a late lunch or something?" Both Fred and Al looked at Jack curiously.

"Well that does sound good," Fred started, "did you have anywhere in mind? Not much to choose from around here."

"Were would you guys want to go? I'm still not very familiar with the town."

"Like Fred said, there isn't much to choose from," Al said, thinking.

"But I suppose one of the better places would be Evelyn's?" Fred suggested.

"Evelyn's?" Jack said, trying to remember why the name sounded familiar, then he remembered. "That's the woman who owns the local bar, right?"

"Right!" Fred said eagerly. "She is! But her bar's also one of the best places to eat in town, too! Well one of the only places actually." He laughed as he corrected himself and looked at Jack and Al, "It's been a while since I paid the young lady a visit, too. I wouldn't mind an excuse to stop by."

"So you guys want to go to Evelyn's?" Jack asked, looking more at Al than Fred since he already seemed onboard.

"Sure," Al said shrugging his shoulders, "I've been meaning to check the place out anyway, but I hadn't gotten around to it."

"Great! Then it's settled. We'll go to Evelyn's," Jack said. "Oh, and lunch is on me today, as thanks for all the help today."

"Really?" Al asked, somewhat surprised. "That's really kind of you, Jack. Thanks!"

"Yeah, thanks!" Fred agreed, then added. "But you know you don't have to repay us for helping you, right?"

"I know, Fred, but I want to," Jack responded. "After all you two, especially you, Fred, have been so helpful and kind to me since I came here. I wanted to show you how much I appreciate all your help. And if either of you ever need anything, don't hesitate to ask for my help."

"Right," Fred and Al both agreed.

All three of them climbed into Jack's truck, but before they left, the three of them looked out at the field and the fence where they had been working. Jack was again struck by just how much they had gotten done, both today and in total. If they were able to keep up their pace, he thought, they could be done all the fences and maybe even start on the barn in a week's time. Smiling to himself, Jack took one more glance at the fence, then pulled out of the driveway and headed for the bar.

Chapter 11: Friends

Jack followed Fred's directions to the bar, as it was off the main road. He was surprised to find that it was close to his farm compared to the other businesses in Claw Creek. It was situated back a winding road that led past several houses and one of the town's newer apartment buildings, which was the closest structure to the bar.

As they pulled into the small parking lot, Jack noticed the building itself was small, and there were no other vehicles in the parking lot. For all he knew, the bar could have been closed. Fred looked at the vacant parking lot with a look of mild surprise.

He checked his watch and remarked, "Huh, could have sworn there would be more people here at this time of day..."

"More like anyone here," Al commented.

"Are you sure they're open?" Jack asked.

"Well only one way to find out," Fred answered, smiling, then he added, "I should warn you two, Evelyn can come across as a bit...rough, but she has a good heart and is really kind once she gets to know you."

Jack wasn't sure how he felt about this new information, but he trusted Fred, so he wasn't about to change his mind about coming here. They climbed out of the truck and headed for the door where a small OPEN sign hung. Fred pointed to it, smiling, and Jack grabbed the door handle and opened the door for them. Both Fred and Al walked in, followed by Jack.

The bar looked just as small on the inside as it did on the outside. Several small tables filled the areas on either side of the door. In the corner to his right, Jack spotted a battered old pool table.

Opposite the door, the entire wall was dominated by a bar lined with stools that looked just as battered as the pool table. Everything in the bar looked old and shabby but also clean and well-kept. If he had to guess, Jack assumed that all the furniture was bought used and cleaned up to make it look more presentable.

Jack saw a door leading into what he assumed was the kitchen behind the bar. Also, behind the bar were several shelves filled with various bottles of liquor and alcohol. Despite its decrepit appearance, the entire bar was spotlessly clean and everything organized and neat.

Behind the bar stood a somewhat short, stocky hyena Anthro. Her fur was golden brown with black spots and larger black patches on her snout and paws. She wore loose fitting jeans and a dark sleeveless shirt. Evelyn looked up from wiping the bar top and frowned at them as they walked in.

"Fred! It's about time you stopped by!" Her voice filled with anger as she spoke, and she dropped her rag on the bar top as she headed straight for Fred, who put his hands up in defense.

"I know, I know, I should have stopped by sooner," he said, still defensive, "but I've got a good reason for not stopping by!"

"Oh? And what would that be?" she smirked, but her voice was still filled with anger.

"I was helping out a friend," he said simply.

"Sounds about right," she said, her smirk changing to a smile as she walked back to the bar shaking her head. "You're lucky I like you, otherwise I'd refuse to serve you."

"I count my blessings every day, Evelyn," Fred responded, following her. Jack and Al followed them as well. "And I don't know what I would do if I couldn't get any of your wonderful cooking."

"Ha! You know I don't do the cooking around here," Evelyn laughed, a high-pitched and very hyena-like laugh, picking up her rag again.

"How is Mel doing these days?" Fred asked without skipping a beat.

"Fine, all things considered," she said, shrugging. "So are you going to introduce me to your friends?"

"Oh, right! Where are my manners! I'm sorry!" he said, clapping Jack on the back. "This is Jack Towzer. He's new to town, and I've been helping him fix up the old farm just outside of town. The one not too far from here actually." Then turning to Al, he said, "And this is Al Knox. He works for Mr. McGregor and he's been helping us with the farm."

Evelyn eyed them both with a scowl. Jack wasn't sure if he should be worried about being kicked out or not. She was a hard person to read, and her inhuman face only made it harder to tell what she was thinking. He could tell Al was having a similar thought as she scrutinized them both.

"New in town and works for McGregor..." She eyed them both closely, looking from one to the other before settling on Al and asking, "You aren't friends with Chad, are you?"

"No! Can't stand him!" Al answered, to which Evelyn smiled.

"Good because he's banned from my bar. My parents let him in here too many times already, and it cost us a lot of money every time. Between the broken furniture, wasted food and drinks, and harassment of other customers. Honestly I don't think the bar could afford another visit from that wannabe Seabiscuit." At her comment, Jack couldn't help but laugh, but he instantly regretted it as she turned on him. "I hope you're not laughing at the fact that my bar is in a bit of financial trouble?" Her eyes stared at him with cold intensity.

"Definitely at the Seabiscuit thing, nothing else!" Jack responded hastily, feeling his heart drop as he was afraid he had just done something incredibly stupid by laughing.

Thankfully Evelyn just nodded and said, "At least you have a good sense of humor..." She shot Fred a look, and he smiled but said nothing. Looking back at Jack and Al, she closed her eyes and sighed, "Well you two seem alright, I guess, if Fred will vouch for you."

"That I do!" Fred laughed. "You've got three new regulars on your hands!"

"I thought you were already a regular," Evelyn shot back. "But if that's the case, Mel will want to meet you. She likes to meet the regulars." She shrugged again, then shouted, "Mel! Got some new regulars out here to meet you!"

Suddenly there was a loud noise from the kitchen, like several pots and pans clattering to the floor. A few seconds later, a tall, thin lizard Anthro came out of the kitchen. Her scales were dark green and were more pointed and jutting on her head and back.

The scales under her chin, chest, and the palms of her hands were a light cream color. She also had a prominent tail that resembled a crocodile's, and her hands and feet were tipped with white claws. Mel was dressed similarly to Evelyn, but she wore a t-shirt instead of a sleeveless shirt.

"Y-Yes, Miss. Evelyn?" she stammered quietly. "D-Did you say r-regulars?"

"Yeah, that's what they said," Evelyn answered, pointing at the three of them. "No need to be nervous. It's just Fred and some new guys."

"Oh, Mr. Nelson! It's so nice to see you again!" Mel smiled at Fred, her timid stuttering completely gone in an instant, and Jack noticed her mouth was full of needle-like teeth.

"Likewise, dear," Fred said smiling back. "These two gentlemen are my friends, Jack Towzer and Al Knox." He pointed at each of them respectively.

"I-It's nice to meet the two of you," she stammered again.

"Nice to meet you, too, Mel," they said almost in unison.

Jack could tell she was nervous when talking to them but not Fred. He assumed it was because they were strangers, which he could understand. After all he wasn't the most sociable person around strangers either.

It was strange though for someone who seemed so nervous to want to be introduced to people. Unless, of course, she was doing it to try and combat her nervousness, or if someone else was putting her up to it. Both seemed likely, and Jack had a pretty good idea who might have been putting her up to it, if that was the case. Mel quickly excused herself and headed back to the kitchen. The three of them took seats at the bar, and Evelyn eyed them as she handed them each a small menu.

"When you've decided what you want, let me know," she said flatly, then she added, "don't suppose any of you want a drink?"

"A drink?" Al asked. "Yeah, water would be fine."

"Water?" she repeated. "Are you serious? Is that a joke?"

Jack couldn't tell for sure, but he thought Al had been serious. Al seemed frozen, not sure how to respond. Was it possible Al had misunderstood her question? The way she asked it had made it clear she meant alcohol, like beer or whiskey. He decided to help his friend out of his predicament.

"He just wasn't thinking, Evelyn," he started. "Al doesn't want any alcohol. It's a little early to start drinking." He hoped, if nothing else, he had deflected her attention from Al to himself, and it worked as she turned to him.

"Yeah, I get it." Surprisingly she smiled, "You guys have been working outside all day, right? So I guess I can't fault you for that, and it is a little early to be drinking."

She set three glasses on the counter and filled them with ice and water. Then she put one in front of each of them and went back to cleaning the bar top. Jack watched as Al smiled and carefully drank from the glass.

He was hesitant to drink from his own as he always seemed to spill it on himself. Despite the risk of making a fool of himself, he carefully lifted the glass to his lips and took a drink. Thankfully he was able to drink without spilling any of it.

But he did notice Evelyn watching him out of the corner of his eye. Jack set the glass down and looked at her. Was she going to make fun of the way he drank? Or say something sarcastic? He braced himself for her next words but was still surprised by her question.

"How long have you been an Anthro, Jack?"

"What? Oh, about three months maybe, why?" Jack responded, not sure where she was going with the question.

"I'm just surprised you could drink from a glass without spilling it even a little. I mean it is one of the most difficult things an Anthro has to relearn, other than walking or driving. I'm impressed that you were able to do it in just three months. Even now I still spill a little every time," she said, and Jack couldn't detect even a hint of sarcasm in her voice.

"Um, thanks?" Jack wasn't sure how else to respond.

"I'm serious, Jack," she said, leaning on the bar in front of him. "People don't realize how difficult being an Anthro can be. So if I see an Anthro do something difficult, and they do it well, I make a point to tell them."

"Amen, Evelyn!" Fred chimed in cheerfully.

They all laughed, but Evelyn's comment had reminded Jack of a fact that he had been avoiding but was unable to forget. He was an Anthro, they all were, they weren't human. Jack wasn't sure why but hearing someone talk about Anthros and normal people had brought his repressed feelings to the surface again.

He sat quietly at the bar while Evelyn talked to Fred and Al. Jack was glad she and Al seemed to be getting along. They ordered their food, Mel brought it out a short while later, and they ate. All the while, Jack sat quietly.

Fred hadn't lied, the food was amazing, and Jack ate it, even though he had lost his appetite. He was still wrestling with his thoughts and trying to hide how he was feeling. It wasn't easy, given how perceptive Evelyn seemed to be and that she was less than three feet from them on the other side of the bar.

Jack noticed her looking at him again, but before she could say anything, Fred asked her, "So, Evelyn, I've been wondering, why is this place so empty? You mentioned money trouble earlier...is it that bad? Where is everyone?"

"Oh, so you noticed?" she said sarcastically. "They're all at The Watering Hole, the new place that just opened a few weeks ago on the other end of town. It's bigger, fancier, and newer than this place. Between them and what Buchannon did...well he got most of us I guess..."

"Ah, sorry to hear that, dear. I know you and your parents worked very hard to get this place up and running. It must be frustrating to see someone swoop in and take most of your customers like that. And Buchannon will be punished for what he did, even if that doesn't help heal the damage he's already caused," Fred said sympathetically.

"Frustrating is an understatement. If it weren't for the few regulars that come in here for Mel's cooking, we would be out of business," she said bluntly.

Fred reached out and pat her arm reassuringly, and Jack went from feeling bad to worse. Here he was, worrying about himself, when Evelyn was going through such a tough time. Jack wanted to say something to

Evelyn to make her feel better. But his words were stuck in his throat, and it was taking everything he had not to lose his composure.

"You'll get through this, Evelyn, and we're here for you if need anything," Al spoke up.

"Right! Exactly!" Fred agreed. "Right, Jack?"

This was exactly what Jack was trying to avoid. He didn't want everyone's attention put on him, not at that particular moment. They were worrying about Evelyn, and he was afraid if he said anything, they would notice how he was feeling. After all he was sure Evelyn already suspected something was wrong.

"Yeah, we have to look out for each other, right?" He managed to get the words out, but Evelyn looked concerned; she had definitely noticed something was bothering him.

"What's wrong, Jack? You look like something's bothering you," she asked, genuine concern in her voice. "You've been quiet for a while, too."

"Nothing. It's nothing, really," he lied, desperately wanting the conversation to end.

"It's not nothing, I can tell," she said, leaning on the bar in front of him again, her face just inches from his.

"I don't want to talk about it right now. It's nothing. Really." He had tried to hide it with all his willpower, but his voice still shook and cracked as he spoke.

Jack felt so stupid. Why was he getting so emotional about this? It was something he hadn't told anyone, even his parents. Up until now, he had been able to hide his true feelings. But now he had lost his composure at the worst possible time, in front of his two new friends and a woman he had literally just met less than an hour ago.

He had to fight back the tears forming in his eyes. Looking down at his hands, he noticed they were shaking. To his surprise, Evelyn took his hands in hers, and he looked up at her. Their eyes locked, and he couldn't stop the tears from darkening the fur around his eyes. Evelyn broke their eye contact to turn to Fred and Al. They had been watching everything unfold in front of them in awkward silence.

She smiled at them and said quietly, "Could you give us a minute please?"

"Sure, no problem," Fred responded just as quietly, his voice filled with concern.

They both got up from the bar and stepped outside. Evelyn watched them go, and as soon as the door shut, she turned back to lock eyes with Jack again. He wanted to die of embarrassment and his chest felt like it was about to explode.

She quietly explained, "I thought you might want some privacy. You seem like you're going through something. I won't push you to tell me what exactly it is, but if you want to, I'm here. If I had to guess though, I'd say you've been bottling it up inside for a while, and losing your composure in front of your friends is only going to make it worse."

"T-Thank you," Jack stammered quietly; he couldn't keep it inside anymore. "I feel like I have to tell someone. So here's the truth: I hate being an Anthro. I know there's nothing I can do to change it, but it bothers me worse than I'd like to admit. Despite every good thing that's happened to me since, I can't shake the thoughts, the reminders that I'm not human anymore. It's like I can't enjoy the good things because of it, and that only makes me feel worse."

"I understand," Evelyn said.

"You do?" Jack asked surprised.

"Yeah, I went through something similar right after I got out of the hospital. Hating yourself, the situation you've been forced into, how everyone looks at you differently and treats you differently just because of something that you had no control over. Then you meet someone who has it worse off than you or who went through more than you. And you feel worse for feeling so bad about yourself. But your suffering is no less or greater than anyone else's," she said smiling.

He felt the weight that he hadn't even realized was there starting to lift from his shoulders and the tightness in his chest starting to lessen. Just admitting what had been bothering him and having someone who understood what he was going through had made him feel better. Jack was desperate to know how Evelyn had gotten over the thoughts and feelings, so he asked.

"How did you overcome it? What did you do to stop the thoughts and feelings?"

"I talked to someone," she answered, looking back to the kitchen. "When I met Mel, I had just gotten out of the hospital, and I was going through the same things you are. In fact when we first met, I compared all my problems to hers, and I decided every one of hers were worse than mine. After all her change was more painful than mine; she lost both her parents to the Virus before she was admitted to the hospital, and her relatives all disowned her after she got out of the hospital. We talked for a long time, and she helped me realize that comparing yourself to everyone else is a never-ending spiral misery and self-doubt. All it does is isolate you from everyone around you. Instead we have to help each other, look out for each other, and not focus on the negative. It isn't easy, but if it was, it wouldn't be a problem."

"I had no idea Mel had been through all that," Jack said surprised.

"Of course you didn't. You barely talked to her," Evelyn said, smirking a little. "But that's exactly my point, you never know how much, or little, someone's going through. That's why we can't compare ourselves to each other. Whether we're Anthros or not."

"I understand what you're saying," Jack said, not entirely convinced.

He understood the basics of what she was saying. Although he just wasn't sure talking about everything and trying not to compare himself to others would solve all his problems. The strange feeling he had had back before he had gotten the Virus was still there after all. Talking had helped a little, but he couldn't shake the feeling that his family would have been better off if he had just died in the hospital instead of becoming an Anthro. Jack hated that thought worse than all the rest, and it seemed the hardest to get rid of, so he asked Evelyn another question.

"So when you said Mel's change was worse than yours, did you mean because of the scales and tail?"

"Oh, yeah. The idea of having hard scales slowly push out of your skin just sounds so horrible. Then to have to grow a big tail...of course you look like you've had some experience with big tails…" she added, motioning to his own tail, "…and then to have scales grow on it, too." She shuddered slightly, "And when I met her, I had assumed that no one could have had a worse change than me."

"Well I understand what you mean," Jack said, remembering how he felt when he heard about Barbara the bat Anthro. "And our changes were pretty much the same, right? I mean we're both canine Anthros."

"Oh, well, yes and no," she replied, clearly surprised and somewhat flustered by his assumption.

"I don't understand. What do you mean?" Jack asked, worried he had said something wrong again.

"Well I guess you could say not all changes are visible right away or immediately obvious," she answered, still flustered, then she pointed to her own tail and added, "plus I only have a little tail…"

Jack wanted to press her further but felt it was best not to pry, as she was clearly not comfortable with the subject. Instead they talked for a while more about Anthros and their experiences before they finally let Fred and Al back inside. Both agreed to keep their conversation between just the two of them and to be there for each other if either of them ever needed to talk in the future.

Chapter 12: Mending Fences

Jack, Fred, and Al sat at the bar chatting with Evelyn and even Mel for a short time when she stepped out of the kitchen for a break. They laughed and joked with one another, and everything seemed to be back to normal. But Jack was still bothered by his own thoughts and feelings, even though his talk with Evelyn had made him feel better.

Every now and again, he would catch her looking at him, but she would look away when he turned to meet her gaze. Jack's dad, if he were here, would probably say she liked him and that Jack should ask her out. It wasn't like that though, and Jack knew she was checking on him to make sure he was still okay. At least he thought that's why she kept looking at him, or rather that's what he assured himself that she was doing.

When it was time for them to leave, Jack paid for their food as promised and tried to give Evelyn a large tip. She noticed, however, and returned most of it. Not before writing her number on one of the bills and giving Jack a knowing look. Fred noticed her do this but said nothing. They promised Evelyn they would see her again soon and thanked Mel for the food, then piled into Jack's truck and headed back to the farm.

The sun was low in the sky as they got to the farm and Al hurried to his car, saying, "Sorry to rush off, but I promised Mr. McGregor I would stop by the store on my way home."

"No worries, Al! Tell Old Man Flint I said hello!" Fred called after him.

"Yeah, no problem!" Al called back. "See you guys tomorrow!"

"See you tomorrow!" Jack said. "And thanks again for all your help!"

Al smiled and waved as he got in his car and drove off. Jack returned the wave and smile, truly grateful for his help and friendship. He turned toward Fred, half expecting him to also rush off, but he was leaning against the side of Jack's truck, grinning.

"You know, Jack, I hate to pry and I won't pressure you to tell me what happened at the bar. But I've known Evelyn since she was born, she's like a daughter to me, and I've seen her turn away every guy who's ever asked for her number. I also saw her give you her number today," he said, reminding Jack of his dad.

"Ah, well, I know what it probably looked like," Jack started to explain, "but it really wasn't that–"

"Doesn't matter," Fred cut him off, "I just wanted you to know how rare it is for her to give someone her number. It doesn't matter why she did it, and I don't need to know the details. Like you said, it probably wasn't what it looked like. If it happened to be what it looked like though, all I'll say is the two of you would make a good couple."

Jack was at a loss for words. He was used to his dad making comments like that but not anyone else. In fact no one else seemed to care if he dated at all, and that was how he liked it. Fred laughed and put a hand on his shoulder.

"Ah, don't take things so seriously, Jack. You're a nice guy. She's a nice girl. If it happens, it happens; if not, well, you've still got a good friend, right?"

"Right, but it really wasn't what it looked like," Jack tried to explain again.

"Well you were acting a little strange before Evelyn asked to talk to you alone, and I was rather surprised she seemed to warm up to you awfully fast," Fred said, and Jack hoped he was coming around to his point of view. "In fact you seemed upset about something," he continued. "Was something bothering you?"

"Well, honestly, yeah there was something," Jack started to explain, but he tried to avoid going into too much detail. "But I talked to Evelyn, and she helped me out."

"Oh, well good," Fred said, "I'm glad she could help you. But you know if somethings bothering you, you can come to me, too, alright? Unless Al or I said or did something to upset you?"

"Oh, no. It didn't have anything to do with you guys," Jack said, hoping he sounded reassuring. "It was...um...personal. I've just been going through some stuff. Probably just stress or something from the quarantine or moving..." he trailed off.

"Right, well, just remember, Al and I are here for you," Fred said, his voice dead serious.

"Of course, thanks, Fred...really," Jack said.

The air around them felt heavy, and Jack wasn't sure if it was due to their conversation or just the setting sun. He tried to think of some way to lighten the mood, but nothing came to mind. Fred stood silently watching the sun with his arms crossed in front of his chest.

After what felt like a long time, he spoke, "I mean it, Jack. You can come to me about anything, anytime." Suddenly Fred grinned and said, "Well I'd better get home! The missus will be wondering what's keeping me!" he laughed.

"Right, thanks again, Fred. See you tomorrow!" Jack said, trying to sound as cheerful.

"See you tomorrow, Jack!" Fred smiled and patted Jack on the back.

Then he got in his truck and left. Jack was left standing in his driveway, alone. He stood there for a few minutes watching the sun set, then headed inside. After he had showered and dried himself off, he sat on the couch and stared at nothing in particular. It had been an exhausting day, both physically and mentally.

He ran through the entire day in his head over and over again; everything almost seemed like a movie. Jack felt like he had watched it all happen rather than actually having been there. The strange feeling from before was worse than ever, too, and Jack still wasn't entirely sure what exactly the feeling was. As he sat there thinking, he tried to focus on it to try and figure out exactly what it was, but all he could decide was that it was a complex web of emotions that seemed to be tied to something involving Anthros. Whether it was himself as an Anthro or other Anthros, Jack wasn't sure, but for now, he would have to be content with his analysis.

Had he really broken his composure in front of Fred and Al? Did Evelyn really sympathize with him? And had Evelyn really held his hands, and had he really gotten her number? It all seemed so strange, almost unbelievable.

Jack also went over what she had told him, and he resolved to do his best to take her advice to heart. Whether it solved all his problems or not, it would at least be a step in the right direction. He rubbed his furry head, halfheartedly wishing it would help him process the day's events better.

The clock chimed and brought him back to reality. It was late, and he suddenly felt twice as tired as he had before. Still thinking about everything that had happened, he headed to bed.

Jack woke up early the next day, having hardly slept. It felt more like giving up on trying to sleep and just getting on with the day. He made himself a cup of coffee and walked outside. Sitting on his front step, he sipped his coffee and observed the quiet of the early morning. It was peaceful in comparison to the events of the previous day.

He sat there for some time before he heard the distant rumble of a truck coming up the road. It was Fred of course, ready to start the day. Jack had hoped for a few more minutes of peace and silence. Fred pulled into the driveway and parked his truck next to Jack's. Smiling as he got out, he greeted Jack with a wave.

"Morning! Hope I'm not too early!"

"No, I'm just moving a little slow this morning," Jack said with a sleepy smile, raising his coffee cup up.

"We all have mornings like that..." Fred laughed, holding up his own thermos of coffee. "The important thing is that we start...no matter how slow!"

They laughed, and Fred leaned on the railing of the porch. Drinking their coffee, they discussed their plans for the day as they waited for Al to show up. There wasn't much left to do after the fences and barn were repaired.

Eventually Al showed up. He apologized for being late, but Jack was just glad he was there. Jack had worried that the events of the previous day might have scared Al away. Thankfully no one mentioned anything that had happened at the bar the day before. The three were able to get to work on the rest of the fences without incident.

Working throughout the morning, they laughed and joked with each other, just like they had the day before. Jack was glad to see that Fred and Al didn't seem to be affected by anything from yesterday. He, however, spent the morning thinking about what he could do differently to avoid bottling up his feelings again and not comparing himself to others. As well as trying to understand the strange feeling better.

Unfortunately Jack quickly realized that the thought he most dreaded remained. Nagging at the back of his mind all day. No matter what he did to try to avoid thinking about it, it was still there. By noon his inability to rid himself of the nagging thought had started to make him depressed.

He remembered what Evelyn had told him the day before, so he suggested, "Hey, guys, it's about time for lunch. Did you want to go to Evelyn's again?"

"Sure! If you don't mind going back that is," Fred said cheerfully.

"I don't mind either," Al added.

Jack was somewhat surprised that Al was okay with going back, given the water incident. They took Fred's truck, as he insisted since Jack had driven yesterday. Just like the day before, the parking lot was empty.

As they walked inside, Evelyn smiled and called out, "Well, well! If it isn't the irregular regular, the water boy, and Jack!"

"Hello, Evelyn!" Fred responded. "So you're giving out nicknames now?"

"Only if they're funny," she shot back.

Evelyn looked Jack up and down quickly, obviously making sure he was still okay. Then went about getting them each a glass of water. Suddenly the kitchen door swung open, but it wasn't Mel who came out. Instead the stranger had large, pointed ears, black fur with a ring of light brown fur around her neck, dark brown eyes, and her head resembled a dog or fox's.

She was carrying a large tray of glasses, and as she set them on the counter, Jack noticed that her hands were very strange-looking. Her ring finger was as long as her entire arm and her pinky finger was the length of her forearm. Both were very thin and folded against her arm with a thin membrane of skin stretched between them. The other three fingers were normal size.

It was obvious, she was a bat Anthro, and Jack's suspicions as to who she was were confirmed a moment later when Evelyn said, "Thanks, Barbara, I can take them from here."

It was Heather's sister, Barbara. He remembered the kind convenience store clerk had mentioned she had a sister who was a bat Anthro. Jack had been wondering if she had accepted Buchannon's offer, but seeing that she was here, he realized that it really didn't matter if it was because of the quarantine or Buchannon. Evelyn turned to the three of them sitting at the bar and introduced them.

"Guys, this is Barbara. She works here on the weekends and when she isn't working at the grocery store. Like she was yesterday."

"Yeah, they needed an extra set of hands yesterday," Barbara added, raising one of her own.

"This is Al and Jack," she continued, pointing to each of them in turn, "and you know Fred of course."

"Who in Claw Creek doesn't know Fred?" Barbara asked sarcastically.

"I'll take that as a compliment," Fred laughed.

"Say..." she said, turning to Jack, "...Jack, right? You wouldn't happen to know my sister, Heather, would you? She's a human, lives in Rawling." He almost flinched when she said "human."

"Actually yeah, I met her not too long after I got out of the hospital," Jack answered.

"Cool, she told me she met a cool wolf Anthro. Nice to finally meet you," she said.

"Nice to meet you, too...small world I guess," Jack added, not sure if she was serious about her sister calling him a "cool wolf."

"Yeah, it really is..." She smiled and returned to the kitchen.

They ate their lunch, and Jack talked with Evelyn for a little while as she put away the glasses Barbara had brought out. He wanted to talk with her about what had been bothering him but decided maybe it was best not to bring it up after what had happened yesterday. Instead Jack told her about their progress on the farm, and she told him about a few of the old regulars that had shown up that morning for breakfast; apparently the Watering Hole had lousy food. Meanwhile Fred talked with Al about getting more supplies from McGregor's to fix the barn. When they got up to leave, however, Evelyn stopped Jack.

"Hey, before you leave, could I talk to you alone for a minute?"

"Sure," he said, then turning to Fred and Al, "I'll meet you outside."

"Right, just don't be too long," Fred responded with a laugh and gave Jack a knowing wink.

Fred and Al walked out of the bar, and Jack found himself alone with Evelyn again. She walked around the bar and sat on the stool next to him. Jack's mind raced with questions, and he found himself surprisingly tense as she sat down.

Had he actually flinched when talking to Barbara? He didn't think he had, but maybe she noticed something? Or was it something he said while talking to her earlier?

"How are you, Jack?" she asked. "I know it hasn't been very long since we talked yesterday, but I thought I would ask anyway."

"Well I've been thinking," Jack started, "and what you told me yesterday helped me a lot. But there's still this feeling, this sense of loss."

"I see, so what do you think you've lost?" she asked.

"Uh, well…"

Jack wasn't sure if he could actually tell her the truth; it seemed like such a strange thing to admit out loud. After all how do you explain to someone that you've lost your humanity? When they have, too?

All of them had. So why was Jack seemingly the only one bothered by it? In the end, he decided he had to tell her the truth, even if he lied, she would probably be able to tell right away anyway.

"I feel like I…no…all Anthros have…sort of…lost their humanity…and it seems like I'm the only one who's bothered by it," he said, struggling to put his thoughts into words.

"Oh well..." Evelyn seemed to struggle with her words as well, "I guess, physically, that's true...I mean we don't look human...and we do tend to use Anthro and human as separate terms when we talk...but well..." she was at a loss for words.

"What makes you human, Jack?" Mel asked, standing by the kitchen door with Barbara, neither he nor Evelyn had heard them come out of the kitchen.

"Just because you don't look human on the outside anymore doesn't mean you aren't human inside. All of us are still human. No matter what animal we may look like now, no matter what we've been through. It's your mind, not your body, that makes you human," she said, her voice quiet but full of conviction.

"Right, and nothing that happens to you can change that," Barbara added. "You're still the same person you were before, or maybe even a better person for it. But you are no less you than you were before."

"They're right," Evelyn agreed, smiling at the other two, "I know you're going through a lot right now, but just remember; you are a wonderful, kind, caring person, Jack. And you have friends that care about you. Not just here in Claw Creek either. There are people that knew you before you changed who still care about you...no matter what you look like now. I'm sure of it."

"I know, thank you, all of you," Jack said solemnly. "I appreciate all your help. I've got a lot to think about. I better get going...the guys are probably wondering what's taking so long. I'll see you later."

He managed a weak smile and walked out of the bar. Fred and Al were waiting for him in Fred's truck but said nothing to him as he approached. Jack climbed in, and they headed back to the farm to finish their work.

They spent the rest of the day working on the fences. Fred and Al joked and laughed as they worked, and Jack tried to join in as much as he could. But he found it difficult as his mind was still trying to process everything the girls had said. His two friends must have noticed his mood but thankfully didn't address it and left him to himself.

As the sun was starting to set, they examined the day's work. Jack estimated that by next weekend they could start on the barn, which he hoped to be done in a few days to a week. With Fred's help during the week, and Al helping out on the weekends, Jack was sure they could be done everything within two weeks.

After Fred and Al had left for the day, Jack went inside to call his parents to let them know what was going on and to see how they were doing,

"Hey, sorry for not calling sooner..." Jack started.

"No need to apologize, dear," his mom said, brushing off his apology, "I'm sure you've been very busy on the farm."

"Not just the farm but, well, I've been making some new friends, too," he said, smiling to himself.

"That's great! I knew you'd meet plenty of great people there!" she replied excitedly.

"So...don't keep us in suspense, son, tell us all about your new friends!" Jack's sad chimed in just as excitedly as his mom.

"Well there's Fred, who owns a dairy farm out here. He's been helping me fix the farm up and he's been a lot of help. And then there's Al, I met him at the farm store, he's been helping me, too."

"That's great!" his mom said, then his dad added, "Yeah, they sound like good people. Hope you plan on returning their generosity."

"Of course, Dad. I have been paying them back little by little by buying them lunch a few times and I plan on helping them out in the future if they need it," Jack responded.

"When they need it, you mean..." his dad corrected him.

"Right, when they need it..." Jack agreed.

"Any other new friends you want to tell us about?" his mom asked, and he hesitated to tell them about the girls at the bar. Jack didn't want them getting the wrong idea or jumping to any conclusions.

However, he relented, and with a sigh, told them, "Actually yes. I did meet these three girls..."

"Three?!" his dad interrupted, but Jack quickly added, "Yes, three, but before you ask, no, I'm not dating any of them!" To which he heard his dad chuckle on the other end of the phone.

"Of course not...you have to get to know them first...then you can decide which one's the one..."

Jack sighed again and said, "Very funny, Dad. But seriously we're just friends, okay?"

"Okay, okay," his dad relented. "Just teasing you a bit, Jack. I have to...I haven't seen you, so I have to get my jokes in where I can."

"Anyway..." Jack continued, trying to ignore his dad's jokes, "the girls all work at this local bar that Fred, Al, and I go to for lunch sometimes. The owner's name is Evelyn, and she has two employees, Mel, the cook, and Barbara, who helps in the kitchen. They're all very nice, and the food there is really good."

"So it's just the food that you're going there for?" his dad asked, laughing, then added, "I'm only joking! I'm sure their all lovely young ladies...and good friends!"

"Right..." Jack said, not entirely convinced that his dad had been joking at all. "Anyway what's been going on back home? Everyone staying safe?"

His mom answered him, "Oh, yes. Not much has changed. Most of the stores and businesses are still closed, and the government is still trying to do everything they can to stop the Virus from spreading. They're putting out new mandates every other day, but I think it's probably not going to be much help with the way things are now. Not to mention that people are rightfully upset about the new mandates and how little they seem to be helping. The news can only blame careless people for so long after all."

"Have there been a lot of new cases in Rawling?" Jack asked, but he wasn't sure if he really wanted the answer.

"As far as I know, I don't think anyone we know has gotten sick," she answered.

"Oh, well good," Jack said, relieved. "I was worried that I had infected you or Dad or someone from work after I got out of the hospital."

"I'm more worried about you, dear," his mom said, a hint of worry in her voice. "Are you taking care of yourself? Eating enough? Showering every day?"

She started to list question after question but was thankfully cut off by his dad who said, "Of course he's been taking care of himself. He's been living on his own since he was twenty. He's fine. He's not a little kid anymore. You're worrying about nothing."

"Oh, so I guess worrying about who our son is or isn't dating isn't worrying about nothing, is it?" his mom shot back.

To which his dad responded, "Alright, you got me there!" he laughed and added, "I guess we both worry in different ways..."

It was Jack's turn to chime in on the conversation as he added, "I know you're both worried about me, and I'm thankful that you care so much about me. But I really am doing fine. In fact the only way I could be doing any better right now would be if you were both here with me now and this Virus would just disappear."

There was a moment of silence on the other end of the phone, then his mom spoke, "It means a lot to hear you say that, Jack. I know you might get tired of my questions and your dad's jokes, but I'm glad you can see them for what they are, us caring about you and wanting the best for you."

"Yeah, well, it means a lot to me that you care enough to worry so much about me. I promise I'll call more often. I don't want you to think I don't care about you two as much as you care about me."

Jack hung up the phone after talking to them a little while longer and concluded that everything was as normal as it could be with his parents. He had no reason to worry, he was sure. After all it had been a few weeks since he had been quarantined, and they would have shown symptoms by now if they were sick. Still thinking about what the girls had told him, Jack went to bed early that night, not really planning on getting much sleep. But he was too tired from the night before and the day's work to try and stay up any later.

He could rest a little easier, knowing that his parents were doing okay. It was one less thing on his mind as he lay in bed. Which was a good thing since he had a about a million questions and thoughts racing through his head that night already.

Chapter 13: News From Home

Over the next week, Jack and Fred finished repairing the fences. They started early every morning and worked late into the evening. On the surface, things returned to normal, but Jack was still wrestling with his thoughts and feelings. He was able to joke and laugh with Fred, and they still made regular trips to McGregor's for supplies where he would do the same with Al.

They also visited Evelyn's for lunch every day, just as they promised. Evelyn and the girls were much harder to convince though, and Jack found all three giving him worrying looks when they thought he wasn't looking. But they didn't confront him about it and took his word for it when he told them he was fine.

Jack also called his parents regularly to check up on them and give them updates on their progress. And to make up for not calling them more when he first arrived at Claw Creek. He also had to endure his parents pestering him about his health and if he had any girlfriends yet. But he endured their embarrassing and awkward questions as he knew they came from a place of love.

He even talked to Mary and CJ during the week. Both had been doing as well as could be expected with the quarantine. Jack answered all their questions about Claw Creek and the other Anthros he had met there. They all agreed that when the quarantine was lifted, they would have to get together to celebrate the farm's repair and so they could meet all Jack's new friends.

As the week came to a close, Jack and Fred actually got the fences done late Friday morning. So they decided to make a quick stop at Evelyn's for lunch, then head to McGregor's to get supplies for the barn. They would start with the roof, which they had realized would need to be totally replaced instead of just repaired. Then there were a few floorboards that would need replaced as well.

They got in Jack's truck, which was backed in front of the barn doors. He put it in reverse to back up slightly, so he had more room to avoid hitting the stack of leftover boards and posts from the fences. Jack had done this numerous times in the weeks previous.

However, this time when he went to hit the brake, his foot slipped and hit the gas instead. Sending the truck crashing into the old barn doors and smashing both to pieces. Jack cursed and hit the brake as quickly as he could.

He put his head to the steering wheel and shouted, "You've got to be kidding me! Seriously!? Why now!?"

He knew why he had messed up but didn't want to admit it. Before he became an Anthro, he would have only had to move his foot slightly to the side to hit the break. But in a moment of forgetfulness, he had forgotten to account for his larger Anthro feet. It was a simple mistake, one he was surprised he hadn't made sooner. That didn't make it any more aggravating, and his turbulent mental state over the last week only made the incident worse.

Jack gave a heavy sigh and lifted his head off the steering wheel. Looking at the broken doors, he saw that they had fallen against the truck's doors in pieces. Fred said nothing, but they both twisted around in their seats to try and see the damage. This proved fruitless though, as they could only see the damage done to the doors and not the truck itself. Seeing no other choice, Jack carefully pulled the truck forward out of the barn and put it in park once it was clear.

They both carefully opened the truck doors and got out. Several deep scratches ran along the sides of the truck. As well as dents from where pieces of the barn doors had fallen against them. The bumper also had a large dent where the doors had hit it. Both barn doors had fallen off their hinges from the impact and lay on the ground in pieces.

Seeing the damage to his truck made Jack sick to his stomach. It wasn't a new truck by any means, and he hadn't paid much for it, but he had gotten attached to it over the years.

He sighed heavily and shrugged at Fred, who shook his head and said, "Well guess we'll have to add somethings to the list, huh?" Jack couldn't help but crack a smile at the hopeless situation and nodded.

"Yeah, guess so..." he agreed, and they both got back in the truck and headed for Evelyn's.

Jack was thankful that the bar had no windows that looked out into the parking lot, so Evelyn and Mel couldn't see what had happened to his truck. But he still found himself telling Evelyn about the incident anyway while he and Fred ate. After their quick meal, they excused themselves and hurried on to the farm store.

The two got what they needed from McGregor's and talked to Al while he helped them load up their supplies. Jack couldn't help but notice Al's expression when he saw the truck. Al tried to hide his surprise and pretend he hadn't noticed it, but it was impossible to miss the scratches and dents. It wasn't until they were done loading everything that Jack filled him in on what had happened earlier.

"We...uh...had a little accident this morning..." he started, not sure how to explain what he had done.

"I can see that..." Al responded, sounding like he wasn't sure what to say either, "...you guys are alright though, right? If it's just the truck that got banged up, then that's not so bad, right?" Jack nodded and shrugged.

"Yeah, we're alright...but the barn doors aren't...I've had this truck for a while, so it's kind of upsetting to see it like this."

Al and Fred both nodded in agreement before Fred added, "Yeah, a real shame, but these things happen. We'll get her fixed up before too long

I'm sure!" He smiled and clapped Jack on the shoulder. "Well! We better get going, right?" Jack nodded, and they waved goodbye to Al as they left.

They spent the rest of the day rebuilding the barn doors, and Jack was happy to see them repaired. It would be easier to forget about his mistake if he didn't have to look at the damage it had caused every time he walked by the barn. Unfortunately his truck would be harder to fix.

Jack looked over his truck after Fred had left for the day. Some of the scratches were light and could probably be covered with a light coat of paint or buffed out with wax. But the deeper scratches would require more than just paint to cover. Aside from the scratches, the dents could be popped out with a suction cup or by hammering them out from the inside. It would take time, but everything could be fixed.

As Jack looked over his truck, lost in thought, he heard his phone ringing from the front seat. He picked it up and was not surprised to see it was his dad calling. Smiling to himself, he answered the phone, happy to hear from both his parents after the events of the day.

"Hey, Dad! You're not gonna believe the day I've had..." Jack chuckled to himself as he said it, hoping to sound like he was taking the setback in stride. His dad cut him off though, and he sounded weak, his voice unusually gravely and serious.

"Sorry, Jack...I don't mean to cut you off but..." His voice trailed off weakly, and Jack's smile vanished.

"What's wrong. Dad?!" Jack asked, suddenly worried.

"I don't want you to worry, Jack...but...your mom and I...we're in the hospital. The doctor says we have the Virus," he replied.

Jack felt his heart jump to his throat and his stomach drop. He was speechless as his mind raced through a thousand scenarios in an instant. Each one was worse than the last.

"Jack?" His mom's voice was on the phone now, just as weak as his dad's.

"Y-Yeah?" he answered shakily, her voice bringing him back from his thoughts.

"Jack...your father and I–" she started, but Jack cut her off.

"You'll be okay." His voice shook even more as he said it, "It'll be okay!

I'll come and stay with you while you're–" It was his dad who cut him off this time.

"Jack...you can't..." He was about to protest, but his dad continued, "...the hospital won't let you in...and you're not even supposed to leave town, right?"

"Right..." Jack said, holding back tears.

"Besides...you've got enough to worry about with the farm...and your mom would be mortified if you saw her without her makeup..." he tried to laugh at his own joke, but he ended up coughing instead.

"Dad..." Jack started, nearly in tears, "...the farm doesn't matter, and we both know Mom doesn't wear makeup." His dad managed a soft chuckle.

"Yeah...I know...and I know you'd be here for us...if you could, but it's okay...we've got each other...You just make sure...that farm is all fixed up...for when your mom and I get out of here, okay?" Jack couldn't hold back the tears any longer.

"Dad, I'm sorry! This is my fault–" His dad stopped him again, sounding almost angry.

"No! Don't you blame yourself...you didn't do anything wrong!" He started coughing again but continued, "...your mom and I...we knew this could happen...and honestly...at this point...I think it was going to happen sooner or later...everyone's getting sick it seems..."

"But–" Jack tried to argue, but his dad interrupted him again.

"No...this was bound to happen I think, and there's...nothing anyone could do to stop it...Don't you worry, Jack. We'll get through this...just like you did...and before you know it...we'll be coming to see you...quarantine or not..."

They talked a little longer before his parents told him goodbye and that they loved him. Jack knew what they were going to go through and that he wouldn't be able to talk to them until it was over. At least that was the best-case scenario, but he couldn't bear to think of the worst. Either way he would be getting a phone call sometime in the next two weeks, and until then, he would just have to wait and worry.

He laid in bed that night going over every time he had been near his parents since he had gotten out of the hospital. Jack knew it would do no good, but he couldn't help but try to figure out when he had infected his parents. Of course he knew they could have been infected by anyone. No one knew exactly how the Virus spread or how it had spread so far and so fast. Despite all the precautions and quarantines, it continued to spread, and now his parents had it.

Jack woke up the next morning, exhausted from another sleepless night but dragged himself out of bed. As he made his morning coffee, his mind wondered back to what his dad had told him the day before. He had said it wasn't his fault, but Jack was sure it was. After all, if Anthros could spread the Virus like some scientists thought, he was the only one who had been close to his parents. Not to mention, who else had he infected without knowing it?

Absent mindedly Jack sipped his coffee and walked out onto the front porch. He surveyed the farm around him and thought of all the people he had been in contact with after he left the hospital. Everyone he worked with at the school, Barbara's sister Heather, and all the random people he had passed on the street.

Jack thought about calling Mary and seeing if anyone at the school had gotten sick, too, but decided against it. Even if anyone had gotten sick, there wasn't anything he could do about it, and he didn't want her to worry about him or his parents. She had enough to worry with the school and the other employees. He didn't want to add his problems to her list of worries.

Also, he wasn't ready to talk about the situation with his parents. It was frustrating, not being able to be with them like they were for him. Jack sat down on the front step of the porch as he finished his coffee and sighed, looking out over the farm again. Strangely he had felt conflicted about the place when he first arrived, despite wanting a farm just like the one he now had. But now he just felt numb, as if none of it really mattered anymore.

He was about to get up when Fred's red truck pulled in his driveway and stopped in front of the porch. Fred jumped out, a smile across his face already. Jack just stared up at him from the step.

"Morning, Jack!" he said excitedly.

"Morning," Jack replied flatly.

"Something wrong?" Fred asked, a hint of concern in his voice.

"Got a call from my parents last night after you left..." Jack started, trying to keep his voice from breaking.

"Oh..." Fred said, the realization dawning on him of the situation, "...ah, they're in the hospital, huh?" Jack nodded, choking back the tears that were forming in his eyes. Fred walked up and put a hand on his shoulder. Looking up at him, Jack could see the concern in his face, despite his bovine features.

"I don't know what to do, Fred," Jack said, shaking his head.

"Not much you can do, Jack," Fred answered, his voice now somber. "Look, I understand if you're not up to working on the barn today. I can come back tomorrow, or the next day, or whenever you're ready, okay?" Jack nodded again.

"Thanks, Fred, but I think I need the distraction right now. I don't want to just sit around and worry all day," he said, forcing a small smile, and Fred nodded in understanding.

"Well alright...so where are we starting today?"

Jack and Fred worked on the barn roof the rest of the day. They pulled off all the old tin that was rusting and full of holes and inspected the roof joists for rot. It took the entire day, but they managed to get it done before it got dark.

While they worked, Fred had talked and joked around like he usually did. Jack could tell, however, that he was genuinely worried for Jack and his parents. It seemed a little strange to Jack, to see someone care as genuinely about people he hadn't even met as Fred seemed to for his parents. But it only confirmed Jack's belief that Fred was a genuine and caring person.

Chapter 14: The Barn and Bar

Over the next two weeks, Jack and Fred, with help from Al whenever he could, managed to replace all the rotten joists in the barn roof and put new tin over it. They also tore out any rotten boards in the hay loft and replaced them. Jack was happy for the distraction from his worrying, but he half expected a phone call any second from the hospital, so he was on edge the entire time.

The work went slowly, as they were working off ladders, and all the boards had to be lifted and held in place to be measured. Next they were taken down to be cut and then lifted back into place. Several had to be lifted and taken down more than once when they didn't fit quite right the first time. After all the roof joists were done, they then had to do the same thing with the sheets of tin, which were very heavy and difficult to handle. Working together and taking their time though, they were able to get it done.

Jack called the hospital every night before he went to bed to check on his parents. It was pointless as their conditions progressed the same as his had and everyone else who had the Virus. Still, checking in made Jack feel a little better about not being able to be there himself. As it drew closer to the two-week mark, he became more and more nervous.

He was also spending more time at Evelyn's bar on days when they were forced to stop early for one reason or another. A few days of rain late in the second week made it difficult to keep working on the roof. Not wanting to be alone with his thoughts and worries, he had gotten into the habit of spending the evening at the bar on those days. Jack found himself at the bar more and more as the two weeks came to a close, no matter how good or bad the weather was.

Evelyn, Mel, and Barbara had been especially nice to him after he told them about his parents. He had even gotten a free meal the night he told them about it, not that he really cared about it, or even ate much of it, but the thought was nice. Jack didn't want to bother the girls with his problems of course, but Evelyn had noticed something was wrong the first time he and Fred had stopped in after his parents had told him.

Despite how awkward Jack felt telling Evelyn and the other girls about his parents, he was glad he had. All three of them had talked with him over the course of the last few days whenever they weren't busy with something around the bar. They were able to help him push away the worst of his thoughts, worries, and blaming himself. It helped that each of them had been through similar situations and scares with their own families.

Still Jack felt a knot forming in his stomach as he sat in the bar on the evening exactly two weeks from the day he had first got the call from his parents. Al sat down next to him at the bar, having just joined him after leaving work for the day. The bar itself was empty, as it usually was this time of day, and they sat in silence as Jack stared at his water, lost in thought and worry.

Evelyn walked up and gave him a concerned look as she set a drink in front of Al, but Jack was lost in thought and paid her no attention. She leaned on the bar in front of Jack and touched his arm. He jumped slightly as he hadn't noticed her in front of him until she had touched him.

Giving him a slight smile, she asked, "Something on your mind tonight, Jack?"

"Uh...yeah..." he answered, not wanting to elaborate, but he didn't have to as she said knowingly, "Expecting a phone call?" He nodded, clenching his jaw, and she nodded back.

"It's been two weeks since they went into the hospital..." Jack said more to himself than to her.

"It must be hard, not being able to be there with them..." she said, then looking him in the eyes, she added, "Hey, just remember that no matter what happens, we're here for you, Jack. All of us..." He nodded, smiling a little, and Al put a hand on his shoulder.

The moment was shattered by Jack's phone ringing suddenly, and both his hands and voice were shaking as he answered it, "H-hello?"

"Hello, Mr. Towzer?" asked the familiar voice of Dr. Hawthorn.

"Y-yes..." Jack answered; he could see Evelyn and Al's concerned faces watching him closely.

"I have good news about your parents. Both are showing reduced symptoms, and I'm confident in saying that they're both out of immediate danger."

Jack couldn't stop a huge toothy smile from spreading across his face as he said excitedly, "T-that's great news! So they're going to be okay!?" He saw Evelyn and Al smile, too.

"Well both are showing some unusual symptoms. We've had a few other patients recently show similar symptoms at this point in the progression of the Virus, and our working theory is that there may be an alternate secondary stage, or variant, to the Virus," the doctor explained.

"Oh..." Jack's expression fell, and he saw Evelyn and Al's expressions fall, too.

"But at this point, all signs point to the variant being survivable, with no alteration to the patient's physicality." Hawthorn continued, "In other words, we believe your parents will not only survive the Virus but will suffer no mutations as well. They will not become Anthros."

"R-really?!" Jack asked, surprised at this new revelation. "That's even better news!"

"Yes, well, we'll need to keep them for observation until they're symptoms are completely gone. And possibly conduct a few more tests to make sure that that is what's going on, but all signs point to that being the case. We'll be in touch as things become clearer."

"Right, of course!" Jack said excitedly.

"I know this is a big weight off your shoulders since you haven't been able to see your parents while they were here and given what we know about the Virus. That's why I wanted to call you as soon as we were sure, but there's still so much we don't know about the Rodrick Virus. I just want you to know that nothing is certain or guaranteed at this point. But as I said, all things point to this being what's going on," he explained.

"Right, I understand," Jack said.

"Still I think things are at least looking up for both your parents, Jack. Like I said, we'll be in touch. Goodbye."

"Goodbye, Dr. Hawthorn, and thank you," Jack replied and hung up, looking at both Evelyn and Al.

"So?!" Evelyn asked excitedly. "That sounded like good news, right?!"

"Yeah, they're going to be okay!" Jack answered, smiling again.

He then quickly filled them in on what the doctor had told him about his parents and their unusual situation. They were as intrigued by the news of a possible new variant of the Virus as they were happy to hear that his parents were going to be okay. Looking to the kitchen, Evelyn then called Mel and Barbara over from where they had been working. Everyone celebrated the good news, and Jack felt the weight of the last two weeks melt away as they all drank, ate, sang, and even danced happily.

Although Jack wasn't normally one for singing or dancing, he was too happy to worry about making a fool of himself in front of the others, but he was glad they were the only ones in the bar. Still he couldn't help but notice the strange feeling he had had for so long was now stronger than ever. Even though it hadn't completely gone away during the last two weeks, Jack had managed to push it to the very back of his mind while he was busy worrying about his parents.

Now that they were seemingly going to be okay, however, the feeling returned to the forefront of his mind. Especially when Evelyn put her arm around his shoulder as she cheered Barbara and Al on as they danced, somewhat awkwardly, together. It was pretty obvious that she had no idea what to do with her hands, and Al seemed like he was afraid to touch Barbara at all. Jack had been so lost in thought that he hadn't even noticed Al get up from his seat. Before he knew it, Barbara and Al's dance was over as the song faded, and they both laughed at their own awkwardness as Al sat back down beside Jack.

Evelyn looked at Jack, and he immediately felt uncomfortable with how close she was to him. Their snouts were just inches apart, in fact if one of them turned too far towards the other, they would touch. He also became suddenly aware of the fact that she still had her arm around his shoulder.

She gave him a wide grin and asked, "Feel like dancing, Jack?"

"Uh...w-well..." he started to stammer a response, but she didn't wait for him to finish as she laughed and pulled him up from his seat.

"Come on! Jeez, you sound like Mel!"

Everyone laughed, even Mel, and they all cheered in much the same way as when Al and Barbara had danced. Although he and Evelyn proved to be surprisingly less awkward dancers than them. Jack was glad, once again, for his fur, so no one would see how red his face was during the dance. Finally the song ended, and Evelyn released him back to his seat. Over the next few songs, each of the girls would dance with both himself and Al and each other.

After some time, Al checked the time and announced that he had to leave as he had work in the morning. Everyone protested, but he insisted he had promised Mr. McGregor, so he reluctantly left after a few more goodbyes. Not too long after Al left, Barbara also departed, stating similar reasons as she had to work at the grocery store in the morning. It wasn't long before Mel also left the bar, giving both Jack and Evelyn hugs before she left.

Evelyn walked her to the door, then turned around to face Jack. He had gotten up as well, not wanting to be rude and sensing that the festivities were over. Evelyn probably wanted to close the bar soon anyway, as it was near closing time anyway.

To his surprise though, she smiled at him, and as she approached where he was standing, asked, "Leaving so soon, Jack?"

"Oh...well...I just thought...you know, it's close to closing time for you, and I didn't want to keep out any later than..." He awkwardly tried to explain his reasoning, but she cut him off with a laugh.

"That's sweet of you but, I was hoping we could...maybe...have one more dance before we call it a night?" She smiled sweetly at him as she took his hands in hers. "I enjoyed our dance earlier, but I was hoping for something a little more...serious?"

Jack swallowed hard and managed to joke, "Y-yeah...we were all being a little silly earlier, weren't we?" She nodded, and Jack had never felt more nervous in his entire life. He could usually tell most girls weren't interested in him, or at least convince himself that they weren't. But he was having a hard time convincing himself that Evelyn just wanted to dance with him again as a friend.

"So you're going to lead this time..." she said, placing his hands on her hips and wrapping her arms around his neck. They slowly moved in a gentle circle around the shabby barstools and worn-out tables. It was less dancing and more slowly moving together, but it didn't matter. Neither he nor Evelyn took their eyes off each other while they danced. All the while that strange feeling that had plagued Jack for so long got stronger and stronger.

Despite how nervous he felt before, as they danced, Jack felt his nervousness disappear. In fact by the time they came to a halt in front of the bar, he was almost upset that their dance was over. Evelyn looked at him with a distant expression on her face, as if she, too, had been lost in the moment.

She smiled at him, and he smiled back, and then she did something Jack had not expected. Pulling him in close, she pressed the tip of her snout to his; she kissed him.

As she pulled back from him, she smiled and said, "Thanks for the dance, Jack. I had a lot of fun tonight, and I think...I think we're all going to be okay."

Jack was still slightly stunned by this turn of events and only managed a simple, "Yeah."

Evelyn sat him down on one of the bar stools and asked him, "Wait here while I close up, okay? So we can walk out together?"

"Yeah, okay," was all he was able to say.

He watched her quickly close down the bar, putting things away, taking out the trash, turning out lights. Normally he would have insisted on helping, but he was in too much of a daze at the moment to think straight. Before he knew it, she was back at his side, grabbing his arm and walking out of the bar with him. In fact he was in such a daze that he almost didn't notice that Evelyn didn't flip the OPEN sign to CLOSED because it already was. Jack walked her to her car, and she hugged him tightly before saying goodbye and leaving.

Jack almost absentmindedly walked over to his own truck, lost in thought. Kissing Evelyn hadn't been his first kiss ever, but it had been his first kiss as an Anthro. What was perhaps the most surprising thing to Jack, other than the kiss itself, was the fact that it felt almost exactly like any other kiss he had ever experienced. All the same emotions, the electricity between two people, it was all there. He got in his truck as his brain tried to comprehend what exactly it could all mean.

As he drove home, Jack smiled to himself. It had only been two weeks, but it felt like a lifetime since he had really smiled. Jack saw his reflection in the rearview mirror, and for the first time, he wasn't bothered by his fur or toothy grin. Not even the ever persistent and confusing web of feelings he had about Anthros could dampen his spirits. Nor did the fact that those feelings had gotten stronger the closer he grew to all his Anthro friends and especially Evelyn.

In fact nothing could ruin his good mood, and he felt a new sense of purpose in his work on the farm. He made a promise to himself that night as he laid in bed; he would finish the repairs on the farm before his parents got out of the hospital and came to visit. The next few days, Jack worked with a renewed vigor and purpose.

He smiled and joked around with Fred and Al more than he ever had before. Jack also talked more with the girls and thanked them all repeatedly for all their help. Also, he talked every night with his parents on the phone as their illness slowly got better and eagerly filled them in on everything he and his friends had done on the farm. Before he knew it, Jack was surprised to find the barn's repairs finished and even a few smaller projects completed by the end of the week.

Fred talked with him about getting animals for the farm. Jack spent the next few days at Fred's farm looking over his animals and deciding which would work best at his. They talked at length about everything from housing and feeding the animals to breeding and raising the young.

He found Fred seemed to be an expert on just about everything that had to do with farming and raising animals. But that was almost expected as Fred had been around it all since he was born. At first Jack had been worried that the animals would be afraid of him because he was a wolf. Thankfully the animals on Fred's farm didn't seem to mind and treated him as if he were a normal person.

Jack also discussed transferring some of Fred's animals to his own farm. Fred had mentioned how he and his family had been helping the Claw Creek community by raising several different animals they normally didn't. The plan being that Jack would take over some of these other animals. Things like chickens, beef cattle, goats, and pigs. After all this was one of the main reasons Fred had been able to help Jack in the first place, so he could ease the workload on his own family.

Chapter 15: Still Human

It took the better part of a week, but Jack and Fred were able to stock the newly refurbished barn with straw, hay, and feed for all the animals that would call the farm home. They had decided to slowly add animals to the farm over several weeks. Starting with the easiest animals to care for and slowly adding the others.

Chickens, being mostly self-sufficient animals, would be the first residents on the farm. They were also the easiest to move. Fred simply penned all thirty of them up in their coop and then carefully lifted the entire coop onto a trailer with his tractor and tied it down. Then they slowly drove over to Jack's farm and unloaded it in its new home near the barn. After it was in place, Jack simply opened the coop door and let the chickens explore the farm on their own.

Jack enjoyed watching the chickens peck around in the yard, and the next morning, hearing the roosters crowing. The farm was starting to feel like a real farm and not just a property. He would spend a week getting used to the chickens before they added the next animals.

Goats would be next, and Jack spent the week preparing for their arrival. Setting up a small section of the fenced in pasture for them to graze in and placing a shed big enough for the five goats to sleep in and get out of the weather when it rained or snowed. Fred arrived at the end of the week with them in a livestock trailer, and Jack helped him unload them in the pasture. The goats took to their new home surprisingly quick, jumping and grazing happily soon after leaving the trailer.

It would be two weeks of caring for the chickens and goats before Jack would get the next to last addition, pigs. Jack had already planned to put them in a small section of the pastures that was almost always muddy and wet. It would be good for the pigs to keep cool when it was hot out. Luckily the pasture also had plenty of dry space as well. Jack and Fred moved a shed into the pasture near the mud but far enough away from it that it wouldn't sink or shift if there was a lot of rain.

Finally, after another two weeks of caring for all the chickens, goats, and pigs, it was time for the final addition to the farm. Jack, Fred, and Al all worked together to corral the ten head of cattle. It was hard work, and the bull gave them some trouble as he didn't want to go on the trailer. However, after some coaxing, they were able to get them all on the trailer. Once at Jack's barn, they then had to coax them off the trailer, which was equally difficult.

The cows would have the lower portion of the barn, under where all the straw and hay was stored, to get out of the weather. Jack was happy to see them grazing in the field and watched the few young calves wandering around with their mothers. Of course Jack made sure to thank both Fred and Al for their help, and the three of them celebrated the delivery of the last of the animals by going to the bar that night.

After he returned home, Jack called his parents and told them all about his day. They also had an exciting announcement. Both would finally be released from the hospital after spending the last few weeks undergoing many tests and waiting for their symptoms to fade.

Finally the doctors were happy with both their test results and their lack of noticeable symptoms. So both his parents would be released the next day, and they were excited to be able to go home. Jack was happy as well, but the quarantine was still in effect, and his parents hadn't become Anthros, thus they would have to quarantine at their home. They would have to wait until it was lifted before they could come and visit the farm that he and his new friends had worked so hard to get running.

Jack had gotten into the rhythm of farm work over the past few weeks, and he felt a sense of calm he had never had before. Not only that, but he felt a sense of purpose, too. He had been to the grocery store and began supplying them with chicken eggs and goats milk. A week had passed since they had delivered the cattle, but it felt like only two or three days at most.

Over the weeks, his relationship with Evelyn had grown as well. He still visited the bar most nights, and Mel and Barbara had caught on pretty quickly as to what was going on. But he had a feeling that Mel, at least, already had some idea. There were even a few nights where she Evelyn asked Mel or Barbara to close the bar for her so she could leave early, something she never did normally. She did this so she could have dinner with Jack at his place.

Even Fred and Al eventually found out about Jack and Evelyn during the intervening weeks. Of course it was hard to hide it when the three of them had stopped in for lunch at the bar and Evelyn greeted Jack with a kiss. Fred simply smiled, but Al's reaction was far more entertaining, at least to Evelyn it was. Luckily for Jack, things returned to normal after Al picked his jaw up off the floor. Jack specifically didn't tell his parents, however, as he wanted to introduce them in person first.

Another thing Jack had come to understand over the passing weeks was the strange feeling, or web of feelings, that had been with him since the beginning. What had been so confusing and strange about it was that it changed and evolved with him. It wasn't a simple emotion or feeling.

Initially, when he had first seen that cat Anthro on the news broadcast all those months ago, it had been simple intrigue. Curiosity about what it would be like to be different. Then after he himself changed, so did the feeling. From simple curiosity to self-hatred, denial of his feelings, and feeling as if he had brought this fate upon himself. Once he started interacting with other Anthros and made friends with them, new feelings of resentment, envy, and confusion mixed with the other things he was already feeling.

Finally, now that all these things were mixing, they hid the underlying cause. They allowed him to lie to himself and deny the real reason he was feeling these things to begin with. When it came down to it, the truth that

Jack had to accept, ever since he first saw that cat Anthro on the news, and the truth that he had been hiding from himself this whole time was simple.

Jack liked being an Anthro, and he liked his lupine features. But it was okay that he liked them, he saw that now because, despite all the terrible things that the Virus had done to the world, he had made the best of it. He had felt like he wasn't allowed to like being an Anthro, that he had to hate it, but he didn't. It was ridiculous to think that he, or anyone else, could be expected to live the rest of their lives in misery because of something that was out of their control. This epiphany helped Jack understand more of his problems than he thought it would, especially when he added it to what he had already learned.

As Jack sat down after another long day of work on the farm, he called his parents as he had done every day since they had gotten out of the hospital. They talked for a while before they informed him that the quarantine was being finally lifted. After much research and tests, the doctors and scientists studying the Rodrick Virus were able to confirm that Anthros were not contagious and didn't carry any active strains of the Virus.

It was some of the best news Jack had heard since his parents had gotten out of the hospital. Jack's parents, they decided, would visit Saturday, and he would invite all his friends for a party to celebrate all their accomplishments over the past few months and an end to the quarantine. He spent the next few days preparing for the party and making sure he invited everyone.

Jack invited Fred and his family, Al and Mr. McGregor, Evelyn, Barbara, and Mel, and Councilor Morgan. He also invited Mary and CJ, if they wanted to and were able to come. But he made sure to tell them that he wouldn't be upset if they decided not to come since the quarantine had just been lifted. They both agreed to come and see what he had been up to all this time.

The day of the party, Jack woke up early and went through his normal routine of taking care of all the animals as quickly as he could. He then set about preparing for the party. It was a beautiful day, so he set up a few folding tables and chairs he had bought under the large shade tree that stood by the farmhouse. Jack chose the tree as it overlooked the barn and pasture where the cattle grazed.

As he was finishing setting up the tables, Fred and his family arrived with a grill and the hamburgers and hot dogs. Fred insisted on setting up the grill and started cooking as his wife and kids helped him. Not long after that, Al and Mr. McGregor arrived, bringing chips and other snacks, and soon after that Evelyn and the girls from the bar arrived with various drinks. Councilor Morgan arrived next, setting a large bowl of potato salad on the table. They all joked and laughed as Fred cooked, and after a time, Jack saw a familiar car pull up his driveway.

It was his parent's car, and he was surprised to see not only his parents but Mary and CJ all get out. His dad waved at everyone enthusiastically. Jack eagerly introduced them to everyone. He found that he couldn't stop smiling as everyone talked, joked, and laughed together.

As everyone talked and ate, Jack looked out over the farm, his farm. He almost couldn't believe it was really his. Jack turned back to the party and saw his family, new friends and old, all talking and eating together. It didn't matter that some of them were Anthros and some weren't. Jack no longer saw the animals or beasts that his Antho friends resembled.

Looking at his own clawed and furry hand, Jack smiled to himself, as he no longer saw himself as the beast he once thought he had become. Mel had been right after all. Despite how he or his friends looked, they were still human, he was still human.

Epilogue: Fate

Francis Rodrick sat handcuffed to a steel chair in front of a steel table in a small plain room. It had been several months since he had released his virus on the world and had been arrested afterwards. He smiled as two men entered, both wore plain black suits and ties. The older man with white hair and a moustache sat down opposite him, glaring at him, while the younger man, who had brown hair and was clean shaven, stood by the door.

"Hello, Mr. Jones...Mr. Smith," Rodrick said, smiling at the younger man first, then the older one.

"Are you going to tell us this time?" Smith asked, ignoring Rodrick's pleasantries, his voice deep, gravely, and cold.

"Hmm? Tell you what?" Rodrick asked, feigning ignorance.

Smith slammed his fist on the table and shouted, "You know damn well what! I'm tired of repeating myself! Every day you sit here and pretend like we haven't been through this ten times every day since you were taken out of quarantine! So...I'm going to ask you one more time! And I promise you, if you don't start talking, I will personally see that you're locked in that quarantine cell again and never come out!" Smith shouted angrily, and noticing a small twitch in Rodrick's face at the mention of the quarantine cell, he launched into another tirade, "Oh yeah! You hated being locked in there for a month?! How about we lock you up in there for a few years?! Or better yet, the rest of your sorry life?! You want to play games and sit here pretending like you aren't responsible for the worst terrorist attack in human history?! You act like what you did was a good thing, but the blood of millions of people's lives is on your hands! No one else's! So I'm going to ask my questions this one last time, and you will answer them! Understand?!" Rodrick nodded, still smiling.

"I understand, Mr. Smith. Please ask your questions." Smith glared at Rodrick as he read out the questions through gritted teeth.

"How are you not sick!? How does the Virus work!? Why did you release it in the first place!?" Smith seethed with anger but took a deep breath and continued, sounding calmer but very tired. "We've been at this for months now, Rodrick, and every day you say the same things, and every day that goes by, more people die. More people are forced to endure horrific mutations that, as far as our scientists are concerned, seem to be irreversible. These are innocent people, Rodrick."

Rodrick nodded and said, "That's true…" He smiled at Smith, "…but what's that phrase you people like to use so much…" he pretended to think for a moment before he continued, "…oh right! It's for the greater good."

Smith frowned at Rodrick's words, then nodded, saying, "Right…'the greater good.' So that makes everything okay? That makes all the innocent people you've condemned to a horrible death okay?"

"It had to be done," Rodrick shrugged. "A necessary evil, if you will."

Smith sighed and asked, "Why did it have to be done? What were you trying to accomplish?" Jones chimed in from the doorway.

"Why? Because they said it couldn't be done! I was trying to achieve the impossible! And I did! And now the world will be a much more diverse and unique place!" Rodrick laughed maniacally.

"So how are you not infected? You must have a way of neutralizing the Virus or a way to make people immune to it?" Smith asked, and Rodrick laughed again.

"There's no way to neutralize it! Why would I have bothered to make a way to stop it? I wanted it to work!"

"Then why didn't you develop any symptoms after the Times Square attack?" Smith asked, and Rodrick laughed again, but Smith continued, "It's been far longer than two weeks, Rodrick, you're either immune or you neutralized the Virus somehow."

"Two weeks?" Rodrick asked, grinning as both men looked at Rodrick in surprise.

In all the times that they had interrogated Rodrick, he had never said anything about the two-week incubation period for the Virus or anything about how the Virus worked. He always dodged the questions or refused to answer. The only reason they knew about it was because that was how long after the attack that people had started to show symptoms. But this was the first time he had mentioned anything about it directly.

Rodrick continued, "You think the incubation period for the Virus is two weeks?"

"Of course it is!" Jones shot back. "It has to be! That's when everyone started getting sick!" Rodrick laughed, and the realization hit Smith.

"The missiles that were launched two weeks before the attack…" he whispered, "…everyone thought it was a computer glitch or malfunction in their hardware that caused those rockets to launch and explode in the atmosphere. Everyone thought it was a miracle that they didn't hit anything, but it was you…wasn't it?" Smith practically shouted the last sentence, and Rodrick laughed hysterically.

"Two weeks!? Ha! You really thought it was only two weeks!"

Smith stood and grabbed Rodrick by the collar and frantically asked him, "How long is the incubation period?!" He shook him violently as Rodrick continued to laugh.

"I never said I wasn't!" Rodrick laughed, then continued coldly serious. "The incubation period varies depending on the host. It could be as quick as a month or…" he looked into the eyes of both the men, "…as long as a year…"

He grinned again and suddenly started to cough blood. Both men immediately backed away from him. Rodrick just laughed again in between coughing fits. Then he looked at both the men again.

Grinning, blood staining his teeth, he said, "What kind of man do you think I am? My goal with the Virus was to infect everyone. How could I not allow myself to be infected? After all I am a scientist, and what kind of scientist doesn't do everything in their power to make sure their work is complete?" He began coughing again, then continued, "I knew there would be quarantine protocols and measures against my creation. That's why I staged the attack on Times Square. Why I timed the release and attack the way I did. And that's why I had to be arrested. To make sure I infected as many of you as possible. You thought you would be safe in here. I made sure you weren't. You're all probably infected right now if you weren't already…"

At his words, Jones suddenly turned, opened the door, and ran out. Smith tried to stop him, but the younger man was too quick. Smith hit a large red button on the wall, setting off alarms and flashing lights, initiating a lock down of the building. Then he turned back to Rodrick, who was still coughing blood and grinning.

"Why are you so sure you'll die from the Virus?" Smith asked calmly over the blaring alarms, putting both hands on the table in front of Rodrick.

"It's been too long. If the incubation period is over a month or two, it becomes more and more likely that the infected will die from the Virus. If symptoms appear quickly, they're more likely to transform. I know exactly how long it's been since I was infected, and it's been too long. My only regret…" Rodrick said, coughing, "…is that I won't be able to see the beautiful new world I've created. But that's how these things go I guess…"

Smith grabbed Rodrick by the collar and looked him in the eyes as he said, "That's called irony…a madman killed by his own creation." He released Rodrick and turned to leave the room. Rodrick laughed.

"Irony? No…I've done such a great thing for this world. It's fitting that I wouldn't be able to see the fruits of my labor. If anything I'd call it fate."

He coughed and laughed hysterically as Smith left the room to report to his superiors what he had learned. After his superiors were informed, they made the decision to only release some of what they had learned from Rodrick. It was feared that if the public knew everything that it would cause a panic.

They would quietly begin lessening certain measures as it had been made clear that quarantine at this point was almost impossible knowing what they did now. The mad doctor would spend the remainder of his days locked in a cell. Eight days after his last interrogation, Dr. Francis Rodrick would be dead. Killed by the very thing he created.